Brown-on-Brown

Brown-on-Brown

A Luis Móntez Mystery

MANUEL RAMOS

University of New Mexico Press ᚎ Albuquerque

Library of Congress Cataloging-in-Publication Data

Ramos, Manuel.
   Brown-on-brown / Manuel Ramos.— 1st ed.
   p. cm.
"A Luis Móntez Mystery."
   ISBN 0-8263-3169-6 (cloth : alk. paper)
 1. Montez, Luis (Fictitious character)—Fiction.
2. Mexican Americans—Fiction.   3. Trials (Arson)—Fiction.
4. Denver (Colo.)—Fiction.   5. Water rights—Fiction.   I. Title.
   PS3568.A4468 B76 2003
   813'.54—dc21

                       2003005782

DESIGN: MELISSA TANDYSH

This is for Max Martínez, a writer and a pal.
Que descanse en paz.

ACKNOWLEDGMENTS

First, a reminder that this book is fiction. Its roots are in my imagination and nowhere else. And, often, the fruit of my imagination has nothing to do with the real world. For example, the legal proceedings that take place in this story, the extended water rights litigation, could not happen in the manner I have described. The case in my story is not based on any actual courtroom drama. I hope that does not distract the reader.

For those who might read too much into my words, I must say that I have nothing but respect and admiration for the lawyers, community groups, organizers, everyday people who become litigants, and their supporters who take on lengthy court battles in the interest of justice, ignoring (and sometimes harming) their self-interests, often at their own expense, and, more often than not, without any recognition. Prime examples are the lawyers, legal workers, activists and the solid *gente* who have been involved in the *Lobato v. Taylor* case, for decades. They are true heroes of the people.

My deep appreciation to the folks at the University of New Mexico Press who gave new life to Luis Móntez—they said yes when no was in the air.

Thank you, again, Mercedes Hernández for everything you have done to help me. Flo, without you this is not possible. Jaden Diego Ramos: you and this book almost shared the same year of birth. May you enjoy a long, fruitful, and happy life.

And, finally, gracias to those of you who asked about Luis. Here he is, one more time.

"*Sometimes I feel like a coiled spring with a dangerous flaw.*"
Attributed to Ty Cobb

"*La verdad padece pero no perece.*"
Mexican proverb

Part One
The Old Man and The Wife

PROLOGUE

Article from *El Semanario*, *"News of Colorado's Latino Community"*
POLICE SHOOTING RULED "JUSTIFIED" BY DISTRICT ATTORNEY
By George Tafoya, Guest Columnist

At last week's press conference conducted on the steps of the City and County Building, Denver District Attorney Daniel Galena announced the findings of his investigation into the police shooting death of Alfred "Freddie" Canales. Galena said that after lengthy questioning of the police officers involved and other witnesses he had determined that officers Gary Brunnel and Lydia Socorro fired in self-defense. On the night of June 17th police officers responded to a call from Margaret Canales, mother of the victim, who called 911 because her son was drunk and violent and had threatened family members with a gun. According to Galena, when the officers arrived at the Canales residence, in the six hundred block of Fox Street, Canales refused to obey their orders to drop the weapon. Both officers fired when Canales raised the weapon in their direction and screamed, "This is it! Now or never!"

Several members of the Anti-Police Crimes Coalition,

many carrying signs reading "Stop Police Murder!" and "Justice for Freddie!" attended the press conference. Robert Salazar, representing the Coalition and reading from a prepared statement, said that Freddie Canales had been "gunned down in cold blood" and that Margaret Canales's version of what happened was "at complete odds" with the "whitewashed cover-up" announced by the district attorney.

Alfred Canales, 25, recently had been released from prison where he served seven years of a fifteen-year sentence for attempted murder. Canales had been convicted of assaulting a man with a tire iron. At his trial, Canales's attorney, Luis Móntez, argued that Canales acted in self-defense. Móntez did not return calls from this reporter.

ONE

MY CHIN SLAPPED against my chest and I awoke with a startled grunt. My eyes blinked open to the soft glare of carefully orchestrated lighting. I recognized the barely audible hum of people leafing through books, furiously scribbling case cites and judicial quotes on sheets of yellow legal pads, or tapping the resilient letters of a laptop keyboard. I realized I had fallen asleep at a corner cubicle in the law library in the basement of the state Judicial Building.

I stretched my arms over my head and tried nonchalantly to survey my fellow library patrons to determine if anyone had noticed me snoozing or maybe had heard snores coming from my table. But I worried needlessly. I almost had the place to myself. Computer research had taken the lawyers out of the law library, except for me. I still did it the old-fashioned way.

Only a few very young lawyers with colorful ties or business-length skirts eyed me disdainfully, even wrinkled their faces. Apparently they *had* busted me indulging myself with a short respite.

Someone tapped my shoulder.

"Móntez? Is that you?"

Harry López grinned like Mona Lisa on meth. I reluctantly shook his extended hand and then rubbed my face to get the blood pumping back into my brain. I had a kink in my neck. I must have been asleep for more than a few minutes with my head twisted in a weird angle.

"You were really out," he said. "I could hear you from the other side of the room."

"What you doing here? I didn't think you knew how to read."

He frowned but his smile almost immediately came back. Harry did not let little things like insults get between him and the rest of the world. Harry had learned a long time ago that a good con man had to know how to get along with anybody for at least a few minutes, even someone who hated him, who wanted him hurt. Harry was a good con man.

He said, "Take it easy, greasy. I thought we were friends, brothers from the hood, and all that."

His smile got even bigger and brighter and I had to turn my face because Harry's brilliant white teeth hurt my eyes.

"Harry, we were never friends and God forbid we're related in any way. I'd have to shoot my father. Me lawyer, you client. Several times. That's our relationship, Harry. Which reminds me, you owe me some money."

His eyes opened as wide as they could without his blue contacts falling out and a red rash of embarrassment crept up his neck jowls and pointy ears.

"No way. Can't be. I paid off your bill, I'm, uh, almost certain. I'll look into it right away, Louie. Honest. I can't believe I didn't finish that up. What you think it is, now? Maybe a couple hundred?"

"Try a couple of thousand, Harry."

The level of my voice had gradually risen. "Thousand" echoed through the large room and bounced back to me, along with a pair of "sh-h-h's" from a worried-looking lawyer and one homeless guy who vigorously gripped a Black's Law Dictionary with callused, short and dirty fingers.

Harry smiled again. There was nothing he could do about paying me a couple of thousand dollars so he had no need to worry about it. A hundred, *más o menos*, now that would have been a problem since we would have understood that such a sum was within Harry's ability. Then the question would have been how he could finagle himself out of doing anything about my bill right then, in the sheltered confines of the library. But for a thousand dollars or more we each had no hope, or expectancy, of ever seeing that much cross over from him to me and, thus, Harry's moral dilemma had been resolved.

I stretched again, shut the casebooks that had not kept me awake and said to Harry, "Follow me."

My work in the library was done for the day.

I thought Harry López was a smarmy lowlife with very little on the ball. My opinion appeared to be the minority one. Harry had survived solely on the strength of his ability to talk his way in or out of situations. Where I saw slick self-promotion, others saw straightforward ambition. Harry was good at double talk, triple talk, back talk, and for that I did not admire him. Yet others thought he was an articulate, loquacious, even earnest young man. By the time reality set in Harry was usually long gone with more money in his pocket than when he had started out, and the mark was questioning whether what had just happened really had happened.

But I gave credit where credit was due. Harry's homies thought he was the luckiest man in the world and I had to admit that the guy led a charmed life. During the numerous times I had represented Harry he had been convicted only once, and that for a misdemeanor harassment charge. Thirty days in the county jail, of which he ended up doing less than half. Not bad for a con that netted him more than ten grand. His rap sheet was relatively short, unlike many of my clients, but of all the criminals and semi-criminals I mouthpieced for, Harry most likely was the real habitual, the genuine article when it came to the practice of blurring the line between a long shot and a downright scam, forget about the difference between right and wrong.

We rode the elevator up to the ground floor and silently walked out of the building under the gaze of the paunchy security guards.

When we were on the sidewalk next to Broadway, I turned to Harry and asked again.

"What are you doing here? What's this about?"

My suit had immediately soaked up the street's heat and I wiped sweat off my forehead.

"Móntez, you're too much. Come on, dog! I could be here doing some work on one of my own cases, couldn't I? It's not unheard of, is it, that a guy checks out his legal situation on his own, rather than turning to one of you ambulance-chasers every time, is it? I could be here in a pro se capacity, so to speak."

"Right, Harry. You're working on one of your arrests. And I'm really Moctezuma's long-lost son planning to take back Mexico."

Harry López could get to me, really irritate me. I just didn't like the man. I grabbed his wrist and twisted it. He jerked and tried to shake me free but I had him good. I twisted some more and he was about ready to drop to his knees when I let him go.

He shouted, "Jesus, Móntez! What's with the rough stuff? You're out of control. For a lawyer, you act worse than your clients. You used to be a mellow kind of guy. But lately, dog, it's like you've really changed."

He rotated his wrist and scowled at me.

"Damn. That hurt. Don't do that again, Móntez. I mean it."

His words came out mean and sharp, and his smile disappeared.

I stepped toward him and he retreated.

I said, "What do you want, Harry? If it makes a difference, I feel bad about twisting your wrist."

He quit playing with his wrist and tried to look me in the eyes, without much luck. I stared at him, waiting for whatever it was that he had to tell me.

"Look, I stopped by your office. That girl you got working there, what is it, Rosa? Now, that is a *large* woman, Louie. Anyway, she told me you were here. What the hell's wrong with that? I need to talk to you, that's all, dog. Just wanted to talk with you."

"So start talking. I'm right here, waiting."

"I thought we were friends, too. Just goes to show."

I didn't respond. My nose picked up the not-so-subtle scent of burning forests. I flicked at a speck of ash on my shoulder.

Smoke drifted among the downtown office buildings like misplaced mountain fog.

Harry sighed, tried again. "All right, look. I got some business for you, if you can believe that. Although, now, I'm having second thoughts. You might not be in the right frame of mind for this business deal."

"Fine with me."

I turned away from López. Before I had managed three steps he was beside me.

"Come on Louie! Sheesh! Get a grip, bro. I got business for you. You too good to take a case nowadays?"

I stopped and again stared at him.

"This better not be one of your usual pitches. I don't have the patience for that."

"No, this is on the level. It ain't for me, see? I got people in the San Luis Valley and one of them, a cousin or something like that, he's in a jam, here in Denver. Needs a lawyer like yesterday. It's a major rap, big jail time hanging over his head. His family knows I've been around and they asked me to line up defense counsel, so I thought I'd see you and arrange a meeting. How about it? What do you say, Móntez?"

I saw that I had a choice. I could brush off López and never think about it again. Or I could agree to help out a man I despised because I needed a new retainer. My choice boiled down to heeding my gut instinct, to respecting my natural aversion to Harry López and whatever he might get me into, or throwing in with him for the sake of the rent on my office and the weekly paycheck I had promised Rosa. Those moments happened in my life, more than I cared to admit. I should have said stay away from me, Harry López. You and your family and whatever strangeness you concoct—stay far away from me.

"We can meet this evening. At my office, around 5:30. And you have to be there Harry, just in case."

"In case of what, Louie? This stuff is getting old. Knock it off. You don't want the job, fine. There are plenty of other shysters around who would jump at the chance to handle this case. It don't have to be you."

I let him finish his rant. I was the only shyster in Denver he could call on cold and not get tossed out on his butt. Unpaid client bills were not that unusual to me but they tended to disrupt the attorney-client relationship of most of my other professional colleagues. Harry López had been a client of several of them at one time or another, and several others had represented his victims in useless attempts to coerce reparations from López.

"Just be there, Harry. What's your cousin's name?"

"Dominic Santos. Maybe you saw the story in the paper?"

Harry wandered off in the general direction of smoky downtown and I walked the few blocks to my car. On the way I stopped at a pay phone and called my office. I made a mental note to look into getting a cell phone.

Rosa answered with her cheery "Good morning, Móntez Law Office." I needed Rosa, it was as simple as that. Smart, dependable, always professional, she managed the office on a regular basis provided I could show her a bank statement on Monday that proved I could pay her on Friday, at noon. There were weeks when my bank let me down and she would not come in, no matter how much begging I tried. She knew my reputation, especially with secretaries, and she allowed no sentiment or generosity to enter our relationship.

"Rosa, dig up what you can on Dominic Santos. He got popped a week ago and I don't think he's been bailed out, yet. I need anything you can find on him. You know the drill. I'll be in later. If you take off, leave the information on my desk. Thanks, Rosa."

I wasted the rest of the afternoon sitting in the Dark Knight Lounge. I nursed bottles of beers until they were warm and watched the new bartender try to improve his standing with a pair of nurses who were giving their tired feet a break. The bartender and the lawyer both struck out. The bartender never made any headway with the nightingales and whatever I expected from the bar and the afternoon alcohol didn't show up.

I had been nasty to Harry López, a guy I normally could shine on like the small-time jerk I knew him to be. Where had that come from?

A few days earlier, Rosa had mentioned that I seemed

stressed and that maybe I needed a vacation. She had been very diplomatic, of course, but her serious tone made me pause. Rosa had too much on the ball to waste her time dispensing unwanted advice. I finished my beer and felt the ache in my fingers from gripping the bottle too tightly. I took a deep breath and released tension from my jaw and clenched teeth.

I didn't think there had been anything happening in my life that could have caused the stress. Not any more than usual. I eked out a living with the down and dirty business of solo practitioner lawyering. I took on the same kind of dead-end cases that I had for years. My clients were triple and quadruple repeats. Low-end gangsters, high-end hookers, and in-between goofs like Harry López. But that wasn't new. That's what I had done since I had escaped from law school and if it wasn't exactly what I had in mind when I first thought that I could be a "lawyer for the people" at least I knew the job and I did it relatively well. Just different "people" from what I had expected.

My love life was nonexistent but that also was nothing new. I hadn't had a meaningful relationship for years although far-away women named Teresa and Evangelina still sent me an occasional birthday card. More to rub it in than anything else, I always assumed. Even the cards had dribbled to practically nothing, probably because I never responded. Somebody told me once that I should figure out this woman thing and I agreed and waited for the solution that never came. My kids and ex-wives had moved on, too, far from any influence I might have over any of their lives. They also sent birthday cards—at least the boys signed a card that arrived in the mail every March. And Jesús, my father, had moved in with my sister up north a few miles from Fort Collins. Out in the country with fresh air and room to amble without being jostled by city crowds and noise, he was a happy man, or so he told me whenever I worked him into my schedule.

To be honest, there hadn't been that many trips to visit the old man. He had found religion and more often than not he wanted to drag me off to a revival so that I could be saved by Jesus. Yeah, Jesús wanted me to meet Jesus. That old time religion had taken root in my father's heart and wouldn't turn him loose. None of that Catholic mumbo-jumbo anymore. Old Testament fire and brimstone had saved my father, a guy I never thought needed saving in the first place. He was baptized again and started telling my sister about the angel who hung around the back yard, and the signs of the approaching judgment day. Wasn't the entire world on fire, weren't we drying up in drought, hadn't the false priests and prophets been exposed as child molesters and sodomites? He regularly reminded me that life on earth was only preparation and I wasn't doing anything to get ready. I never asked what I had to prepare for but I sensed it involved flying squads of angels ambushing the hordes of hell in the final battle between good and evil. I hadn't seen Dad's evangelism coming but when it happened I wished him well and respected what he had chosen for himself. He was the smart one in the family and I calculated that in his final years on earth he must have realized a bit of truth that so far had escaped me and I would, therefore, give him much more than the benefit of the doubt.

But nothing seemed to get at the heart of what might be "stressing me out", as Rosa had put it.

The juke box played a Dwight Yoakam song. Turn it on, turn it up, baby. Turn me loose. A honky-tonk number in a honky-tonk bar for what had turned into a honky-tonk afternoon. That deserved another beer, at least. By the time I left for my appointment with Harry López and his cousin's family, I hadn't overcome my general malaise but I sure had spent a lot of money on country music.

TWO

HARRY INTRODUCED HIS uncle Fermín Santos and a woman named Mariele Castilla. The tall, robust man had to be in his seventies. A deep tan, strong hands, and a rigid politeness fit in perfectly with his crisp jeans, polished cowboy boots and pressed flannel shirt. He fidgeted with a set of keys and I took that as a sign that he was a troubled man, worried for his son and a bit angry that he had to talk with an attorney about his family—a man who expected to have things his way.

No one told me Ms. Castilla's connection to the family or the potential case. She sat in one of my office chairs next to the old man, holding his hand, much like a daughter. Harry sat in the background trying to be inconspicuous but his bothersome smile occasionally intruded into the room.

After they accepted my offer to have Rosa bring them something to drink, the uncle began to explain his understanding of what had happened to his son. I interrupted him.

"Wait. Please. Before we start talking about Dominic's case, I have to get something cleared up. I am assuming that you are here to explore the possibility of hiring me to represent your son, Mr. Santos. In that connection, I will need to interview you, and then your son, of course. At this point it is important to establish an attorney-client relationship so that what we say here remains confidential. In other words, for your and

Dominic's protection, I can't divulge to anyone what is said here unless you tell me it's all right. Is that clear?"

The man nodded.

"Yes, of course. I've had to deal with lawyers before. I understand."

"Good. Then I will have to ask Harry and Ms. Castilla to step out to the waiting room. Right now, you are my client, Mr. Santos, and maybe your son will be, too. If need be, I can talk with Harry and Ms. Castilla later. But if we don't establish this confidential relationship now, there may be some problem later. It's a bother, I know, but it's the way we lawyers have to work. It's in your best interests and those of your son."

Santos shook his head.

"No, no, Mr. Móntez. Mariele is my son's wife. Surely she can stay here to talk about her husband, no?"

I looked at the woman closely for the first time.

I had heard the *chisme*, the silly gossip, about me and my problems with women. I did have to admit my track record was not good—two failed marriages and a broken heart so many times that I could have starred in my own *telenovela*. But those private wars had me wary and jaded and the last thing I needed was an entanglement of a personal nature.

So I looked at Ms. Castilla without any hidden agenda, without any preconceived notions, without sex in the back of my mind. I saw dark hair pulled back and held in place with a silver and turquoise barrette. Her slender, taut face had a pained expression that I assumed had been produced by her husband's predicament. She also wore jeans and a western shirt and scuffed boots. She was as country as the music I had been listening to only an hour before.

"In that case, she can stay. Harry, you have to wait outside."

I had made Harry come to the meeting and just as quickly as I could I wanted to get rid of him.

The con man stood and bowed to his relatives like a geisha greeting customers.

"I'm going to take off anyway. My uncle and Mariele have their own ride and I have to deal with business. Thanks, Louie. I owe you one, dog."

I wanted to say, you owe me two thousand, Harry. The uncle and the wife thanked him profusely for his help and then the little weasel was gone.

Santos's voice carried well in the confines of my small office. The story came slowly at first before it burst from him in a cascade of emotions—anger, hurt, confusion.

"My son has always been a bit wild, Mr. Móntez. Some of that is my fault, of course. I had to raise him myself after his mother died when he was just an infant. But I had a ranch to operate and I did not spend as much time with him as a father should. My sisters and their daughters helped and they did what they could, but by the time Dominic was in his teens they couldn't handle him and it was too late for me to try to exert any control. He left the house to be on his own when he was only fifteen. Until he met Mariele he was in constant trouble with the law, or other people. In Mora, a man tried to kill him. Dominic spent four years in the New Mexico penitentiary because he went too far when he defended himself. But, like I said, that was before Mariele made him settle down. She has been the best thing that ever happened to him."

I expected the woman to blush or roll her eyes or show some sign that the man overstated her role in the bad seed's conversion. She patted the old man's hand and watched me.

"After Mariele moved in with Dominic in the *casita* I had given him, he quit carousing, running around, drinking. It's been at least two years since he's been in any kind of trouble. He's my ranch foreman, and one day I expect that he'll run the entire operation. The ranch will be his when I'm gone. It's not much, of course, but we have some range land that we lease out, and we do some farming. We own a few horses, cattle, goats. I had taken him out of my will during all his troubles, but now he's proven he is a man and that he can handle it. But . . . this latest. I just don't know." He caught himself and reeled in his doubt. "He didn't do it! He couldn't have!"

As he talked, I leafed through the file of newspaper clippings that Rosa had organized for me. Headlines gave me quick summaries.

ARSON SUSPECTED IN FIRE NEAR
HISTORIC SAND DUNES.
EX-CONVICT LINKED TO THREATS.
CBI BLAMES ARSON PLOT ON
SAN LUIS WATER WAR.

Each news story mentioned Dominic Santos's record of arrests and the conviction for assault. One of the papers printed a mug shot photograph of the accused. There were definite physical similarities between the father and son. Dominic was described more than once as a man "known for his temper." He would stay in the Denver jail until a cop from the valley had the time to venture to Denver to pick him up. No one seemed to be in a hurry for that.

Ms. Castilla picked up where the old man had finished.

"You understand, don't you Mr. Móntez, that in the valley, there is nothing more valuable than water?" The husky voice was almost hoarse. Her words were quick, effective. "We live in a beautiful part of the state but it has no industry to speak of. People survive on small farms and ranches or in the small businesses in the small towns. Thousands of tourists pass through the valley but they don't spend much money except for maybe a tank of gas or a ticket on the narrow gauge railroad. We've always been poor in terms of income and material wealth but we're rich in history and traditions. We're trying to keep what we have but there are others who don't care, who only see opportunities to make money even if it means hurting the people of the valley, or destroying the valley itself."

I knew the story. Chicano History 101 —*raza* ripped off again. For generations the water in the valley had been exported to other parts of Colorado and even to California and other states. The developers claimed water rights under deeds, contracts and other documents that people signed years ago without understanding them, without realizing that they were giving away the future of the valley.

Rosa appeared with a tray of glasses and a pitcher of iced tea. This week her hair color happened to be a shade she had informed me was cranberry. Rosa kept the place from going stale.

I took advantage of the break to skim an article Rosa had found in one of the Sunday inserts about the water dispute that had torn apart the close-knit valley community. She had circled with red ink a quote from a man named Matthew Barber.

The San Luis Valley can look harsh and dry to many people. It's a high mountain valley with stretches of semi-arid desert. The Great Sand Dunes are the tallest sand dunes in North America and they are growing, expanding every year. The wind storms are notorious, as are the sub-zero winters. And yet, beneath the valley sits a two billion acre-foot aquifer. One acre-foot equals more than 300,000 gallons of water. That's enough water to support a family of four for a year. That's a very valuable resource, both in terms of what it could mean to the environment and lifestyle of the valley, and what it could mean in dollars. Millions of dollars.

Rosa exited and for a few minutes no one said anything. The old man's image of strength gradually had receded as he and his daughter-in-law had revealed his son's plight.

Mariele Castilla stared at her lap and breathed quietly. I assumed that the father and the wife finally had allowed the reality of Dominic's trouble to set in, to take hold, and now they were overwhelmed.

I said, "What's your husband's connection to all this? What do the charges against him have to do with the San Luis Valley aquifer?"

She stirred herself and made a motion with her hand that could have been the wiping away of a tear, if she had been crying.

"Dominic is accused of threatening Matthew Barber and then of burning down a cabin owned by Barber, on Barber's ranch. A man was killed in the fire. The police are saying the fire was aimed at the Sangre de Cristo Water Company."

She spoke as though she were reciting names in a phone book. The raspy voice did not break. Ms. Castilla kept herself in check, did not give in to any emotion or fragility although she had to describe the tragedy that had struck her husband and her husband's family.

I wrote down what she said but I was more interested in how she said it. I added the words "felony murder" to my notes.

She continued, "The Sangre de Cristo Water Company is the biggest water thief in the valley. Matthew Barber *is* the Sangre de Cristo Water Company."

The old man jumped to his feet and leaned over my desk.

"*¡Cabrones!* The fucking water company is behind all of this! It's their damn fault. That coward Barber is the one!"

He raised his fist in my direction but it had to have been meant for the cursed water company. Spittle dribbled from the corner of his mouth. I shook my head in reflex and tried to catch the woman's eye to make sure that the old man was all right. Santos, even at seventy, was an imposing man.

"Easy, Mr. Santos. Sit down. Don't get excited."

He ignored me. "Barber and his thugs are destroying the valley! He's destroying me! He's robbing me of everything I've worked for my entire life. If I'd had the balls I would have killed him myself years ago." His fist punched the air. "But I thought that it would work out. Everyone told me to be patient, to give the system time to fix what was wrong. They told me the laws would protect us. I trusted lawyers and judges and courts. And what did it get me? *¡Mierda!* And now my son is accused of murder! The only murderer is Barber! I'll kill him! I'll kill the sonofabitch!"

He coughed and jerked in spasms. He clutched his chest near his throat then fell forward and hit his forehead on the edge of my desk. He rolled off the desk and onto the office carpet. I rushed to him from behind the desk. Mariele Castilla knelt next to the old man. She took a bottle of pills from his shirt pocket and placed a pill inside his mouth.

"Get some water. Hurry! And call an ambulance."

I had Rosa call for help while I filled a glass with water. Ms. Castilla reacted to the old man's attack much better than I did. She wiped blood from his forehead and soothed him while we waited for the ambulance. I was useless and in the way. I felt like a stranger in my own office.

She talked to him quietly.

"It will be all right, Fermín. Dominic will be okay. Don't worry about him, about any of this. It will be okay."

The old man's breathing returned to normal but he appeared to be passed out. When the ambulance attendants rushed in my office she told them that Santos suffered from angina and acute anxiety attacks. She showed them the bottle of pills and then let them take him away. She hurriedly told me that she would get back to me as soon as she knew he was going to be all right. Then she was gone.

Rosa stood next to me in the doorway of my office, tapping her foot. She said, "I hope he's going to be okay. What did you say to get him so upset?"

The ambulance sped down the street and Mariele Castilla screeched away in a new pickup.

"Please, Rosa, I had nothing to do with the old man's attack."

"Right, Louie."

"I'm serious. Santos is sick, obviously, and talking about his son and his son's trouble worked him up over the top. There's a lot of pent-up anger, even hatred, in that man. If any of it rubbed off on his son, then Dominic Santos is probably guilty of everything he's been accused of, and more."

"The woman handled it well, don't you think? She's what, the wife?"

"Yes. And you're right. She was cool. Like she'd been through it before."

"Makes sense."

We began our regular routines for closing the office for the day. As Rosa straightened out the waiting room I returned files to a filing cabinet. I wiped a spot of blood off the edge of my desk with a tissue.

In a few minutes Rosa ran out of the office hollering "Goodnight, Louie" over her shoulder. I had not found the right moment to ask if she had noticed Mariele Castilla's scarred wrists.

THREE

I STAYED AT the office and read through more of the newspaper stories and reviewed notes of my conversation with
Fermín Santos and Mariele Castilla. I caught up on all of Rosa's
groundwork. I was trying for the big picture before I got swallowed by the inevitable details that crept into every murder
case. Dates, times, names, addresses, telephone numbers, and a
thousand more facts would swarm around me like maggots on
a moldering corpse.

I planned to trek to the county jail and talk with the notorious Dominic Santos first thing in the morning. The old man
had not denied that his son had committed the crimes he had
been accused of, nor had the wife professed her husband's inno-
cence. They had left the impression that whatever Dominic
had done, it had been with good reason. It was all the fault of
the big bad water company.

I flipped through my overflowing Rolodex for the number
of my nephew in La Jara.

The woman who answered called Michael Torres to the
phone. We exchanged the small talk of relatives who rarely
contact each other. Michael knew I wanted something as soon
as his wife had told him who was calling and I got to it as soon
as I had moved past the good manners.

"Michael, what can you tell me about Fermín and
Dominic Santos and Michael Barber, and all that water

war nonsense going on down there? Just how serious is this thing?"

He answered quickly. "About as serious as any other war, Louie. The Santos family is one of the oldest valley families, and when I say old, you know that there are some people here who trace their roots in this part of the country more than two hundred years. Fermín is one of the real old timers, a symbol of the old ways, the old culture. He's also very wealthy, at least by valley standards. He owns a huge stretch of land that butts up against the Sand Dunes, and up against the land owned by the Sangre de Cristo Water Company, what they call the Grande Vista Rancho. He's been fighting for water rights against the water company for decades. But he lost in the courts over the years and recently he lost his appeal in the federal court. What it means is that the water company can export hundreds of thousands of gallons of water to paying customers along the front range, maybe out of state. They made a killing. As for Santos, the water he needs for his own operation will be way down, especially now with the drought, except what he can import himself or tap into from some other source. Ironic, since his land sits on a massive lake of water. But it all belongs to the water company, and Matthew Barber. At least that's what the courts said. No one's convinced the old man, yet."

I scribbled as he spoke. I asked him, "You think the old man or his son would do something extreme, like the fire? Man, that's just crazy, the way things are so dry around the state. Sounds like the old West, except it's not sheep herders and cattlemen."

Now Michael paused. "Louie, I have to tell you about that family. There's plenty. They may be part of the history of the valley and they may be respected for the fight they've led against the water company but, to tell the truth, it's a toss-up between who's hated more, Matthew Barber and his rowdies or the Santos family. Especially that Dominic Santos, Louie. He's a real bad one. No one's sorry to see him locked up. And the father's made his *own* enemies over the years. He can be heavy-handed in business. He's got his own deal cooked up with another water outfit but that won't fly now that the court's cut him out of the picture."

I wrote the words *hated* and *water rights* and *court order*. I offered my own insight.

"There's always two sides."

Michael laughed then said, "At least, *tío*. And in direct answer to your question, I guess we all thought Dominic Santos was guilty of everything he's been accused of, and more. I've had my own run-ins with that guy and it wasn't pretty. Guys like me, we sit back and watch the big boys fight out this water war and for all we care they can run each other out of business and out of the valley. In the end, it's still going to be the same old valley and the *gente* like me, we're going to survive, and one way or another we're going to get our water and our grazing rights and our kids are going to get decent schools, and one of these days some of us will even get good jobs. It's just the way it has to be down here. You know the valley *gente* , Louie. Tried, but true."

Yes, I knew plenty of valley people and I knew the valley rap. I also knew that no matter what Michael said, the "valley *gente*" included good and bad, honest and crooked, just like any other group of people in the world.

"One more thing, Michael. How about Dominic's wife, Mariele Castilla? What's her story?"

Michael's pause wasn't pregnant, exactly, but it sure missed a period or two.

"I have to be careful what I say about that woman. My wife thinks that we had a thing going a while back. It's not true, Louie, but that's the way Mariele is thought of. And she's not Dominic's wife, although the old man wants it to be that way. Dominic and Mariele shack up some of the time, when they're not screwing around with somebody else, or they're not trying to kill each other over at the Roundhouse Bar. The fights those two have had are famous, even for the valley. She showed up here a few years ago and made it clear she was looking for someone to take care of her. A lot of guys jumped at the chance, Louie, including Dominic Santos."

So much for the old man's belief that Ms. Castilla had tamed Dominic and his wild ways. I played a hunch.

"And Matthew Barber? Was he on her dance card, too?"

"You got it, Louie. That's over, but when it was on it was real hot and heavy between those two. I'll tell you, *tío*. You're in with quite a group. Watch your back, that's all I can say."

!!!

Mariele Castilla called and asked if we could get together to talk. I pretended that I had expected her call and then I proceeded to the Dark Knight, where we had agreed to meet. I left my office around ten-thirty, tired, hungry, anxious, with a budding headache from the interrupted afternoon beer—the right conditions for an all-time great drunk.

Monday nights were quiet in the Dark Knight and the bar sat halfway between my office and the hospital, so it made a certain kind of sense to Mariele Castilla for us to meet there, and I needed a drink, so it made all kind of sense to me.

!!!

For the second time that day I studied the face of Mariele Castilla but it must have been the thousandth time in my life that I sat in a bar across from a woman I found attractive, not sure what I was doing there and in the dark about her motives. Only rarely had those times worked out for me.

I quickly drank some scotch and ordered another. The kink in my neck had returned and I had trouble sitting still while she talked. I could feel the tightness in my jaws again and the Dewar's hadn't relaxed me.

She informed me that Fermín Santos had suffered an attack of angina and a minor concussion and would have to stay in the hospital for at least another day.

"At his age," she explained needlessly, "the doctors don't want to take any chances."

I nodded.

"All of this business with the water company, and Barber and Dominic. I'm afraid it's hurt Fermín more than he wants to admit."

"How is Dominic? Did you get a chance to visit him?"

She swirled her drink.

"Actually, no, not since we got here in town. We were going to stay with some old friends of the family. We drove down from the valley, went by their house, then met with you, then Fermín had his accident. It's too late, now, to visit Dominic. I'll go by the jail tomorrow morning. Maybe I'll have some good news about his father."

"Let's hope so. He seems like a strong man. Just too much all at once, I guess."

"Yes, the court decisions and Dominic's arrest, all happening at once. Just too much for him."

"Why does the old man call you Dominic's wife? You're not married, are you? Or is it common-law?"

It could be almost impossible to see details in the Dark Knight Lounge. The lighting was always subdued and when the place was busy clouds of smoke added to the heaviness and the lack of light. Corners of the small dance floor disappeared, and couples sitting in one of the booths near the back felt safe that no one else would see them. The narrow hallways to the restrooms were bleak and dangerous-looking because they were as dark as the alley behind the building.

But I saw the look of surprise that crossed her face, followed by a smirk. She stared at me, waiting for me.

Harry López had accused me of being "out of control." I didn't feel out of control but the woman's reaction told me that I had stepped over some line she had drawn between us.

I said, "I apologize if that sounded rude. It's in my nature to ask impolite questions, I guess. If I'm to be Dominic's lawyer I have to know everything about the family that might help me with Dominic's defense. Whether you or Dominic are actually married seems like something I should know."

"Yes, Mr. Móntez, it sounded rude. It *was* rude. I didn't want to meet you tonight to talk about my marital status or anything else personal. I wanted to go over Dominic's case. We didn't get much done at your office, if you will recall."

"Right. And we have to do that. Go over the case, I mean. So, are you married to Dominic or not?"

Mariele finished her drink, set the glass aside and said, "Very well, Mr. Móntez. If you insist on getting into this. We are not married. Mr. Santos, Dominic's father, wants us to be married. He thinks it would be the best thing for Dominic. So far, it hasn't happened. And, no, we don't think we are common-law married either. When you talk with Dominic he'll tell you the same thing. I wasn't trying to keep that from you. I have no reason to. I just didn't want to contradict Fermín. In his eyes, we are married. That's the way he thinks."

I didn't lecture her about the attorney-client privilege and confidentiality or having trust in your lawyer. It was easier to let it go, to believe her and move on. I wanted to believe her. I listened to her speak and I thought that I liked how her lips formed words. I liked the way her slow voice moved around the booth and how it sounded tough and weak at the same time. I told myself that I was starting to like Mariele Castilla even though she had not been straight with me, almost from the first minute she had met me.

"Let's start over, Ms. Castilla. What do you know about what happened between Dominic Santos and Matthew Barber?"

She let go of the tension I had created and answered, "If he had done what they say, Dominic wouldn't have run to Denver. He got arrested in this town because he was up here on business for Fermín. If Dominic needed to run, he would have made for the mountains, for the high ground where he could survive for weeks. No one in the valley would track him down. No one would want to. He could live up there until winter, and then make his way south, to New Mexico, where he has friends who would hide him. So, coming to Denver after the fire doesn't make any sense."

"In your way of looking at things, I guess not. But it's not enough."

She nodded in agreement. "The real reason I know he didn't do it, is that he just isn't capable of doing what they accuse him of. Oh, not that he wouldn't want to hurt Matthew. Everyone in the valley will tell you that. Dominic won't deny that. But setting fire to the Barber cabin? We all know the risks to everything that a fire can cause. It was a stupid act. And for what? To get at Matthew doesn't make sense. Dominic's not that, uh, not that indirect. Setting a fire just isn't his type of thing. Dominic would find Matthew and personally confront him. He'd beat the hell out of him, if you want to know the truth, Mr. Móntez. This

23

fire is almost too obvious. Whoever set it, it wasn't Dominic. Of that I am absolutely sure."

The faded bar light danced across her face and the reflection from the juke box made her eyes shine with streaks of blue, red and yellow. Her hands kept busy while she talked. Her fingers rubbed the cuffs of her shirt, finally working themselves under the cloth where she slowly, methodically massaged her wrists. She described Dominic's choices of mayhem with clarity and some excitement.

I continued to drink as I listened to her but I was distracted from her story by the motion of her fingers under the sleeves of her shirt. As far as I could tell, she was not aware of that motion.

I asked, "You're saying that you don't think Dominic set the fire because it's not violent enough, not direct enough?"

She shrugged. "If you want to put it that way. I know Dominic, Mr. Móntez. I know what he's capable of, how he thinks. In his eyes Matthew Barber and the water company are the enemies of his father. He thinks of them as forces trying to ruin Fermín Santos. Therefore, they are *his* enemies. Whenever Dominic has had to deal with people he thought of as enemies, he's taken them head-on, up front and without any qualms. One-on-one and as personal as he could make it."

She closed her eyes, tightly, as though the glare of her revelations about the man she lived with had become too much for her. She stopped rubbing her wrists.

She said, "Even the New Mexico state prison couldn't change that about him. He ended up behind bars because of that attitude and he never regretted what he did, never said he made a mistake. No, Mr. Móntez. Dominic Santos didn't burn down Matthew Barber's cabin. If Matthew had been beaten or shot while he rode across his ranch, I might not be here asking you to represent him. I might be begging you to do everything in your power to keep him in jail because he's a wild animal that needs to be caged."

The way she said it, mixed in with the day's drinking and all that had gone on in my head for the past few weeks, I couldn't be sure that she hadn't asked me to do exactly that.

She fiddled with a purse and eventually produced an envelope. She handed it to me and said, "Fermín intended to give this to you today. If it's not enough for a retainer, we can get you more. We want you to be our lawyer."

I opened the envelope and retrieved a check for ten thousand dollars signed by Mr. Santos.

I said, "It's enough to get started. We will have to sign a retainer agreement, be clear about what you expect from me and what I expect from you. But, officially I am now working for you, Mr. Santos, and Dominic."

We talked for several more minutes and I picked up details about the charges against Dominic and about Kyle Alarid, the water company employee who had been in the cabin the night it burned. Alarid's death made Dominic's case a potential capital offense and I told her that no matter what the truth turned out to be, it was bound to be a difficult, complicated trial. I also reassured her that I would visit Dominic in the morning.

"Maybe I'll see you there," she said as she left the bar.

To her back I said, "Yeah. Maybe."

⁝⁞

Mariele Castilla left the Dark Knight Lounge at midnight. I stumbled out of the joint about an hour later. The drive home was quiet and uneventful, as far as I remember.

I couldn't sleep, couldn't stay completely awake. I plopped myself in front of the television and flipped through the cable channels. For a few minutes I watched an old Bogart flick, one that I had enjoyed before, but it only deepened my depression because I couldn't stop thinking that everyone in the movie was dead, and no one made movies like it anymore.

I had opened a beer but I ignored it, for the most part. My mind was caught up in the constantly changing pictures on the tube, the bits and pieces of conversations, commercials, announcements, news briefs.

The man on the television said, "We have an update on a story that we reported earlier. The Denver County Sheriff's office has just released a statement that a fight between two inmates escalated until more than twenty prisoners were involved in what the spokesman for the Sheriff's office described as a 'bloody free-for-all.' At least a dozen prisoners suffered serious injuries, as well as four guards who had to be rushed to emergency care. As we reported during our ten o'clock broadcast, a prisoner was killed in the melee. We have now identified that prisoner as Dominic Santos. Santos was the San Luis Valley man arrested in connection with a fire that caused the death of one person and thousands of dollars of property damage. Santos had been in the Denver jail awaiting transport to Alamosa."

I expected more but the news man had nothing else to give. I roamed through other channels and found the story repeated without any additional information. Finally, I clicked off the set and let my body sink into the lumpy cushion of my recliner. The kink in my neck had untied itself but new aches and pains had sprung up out of nowhere to torment my body.

The screen continued to glow in the darkness. The gray ghost waited for me to do something. I sat there through the night, sometimes sleeping, weaving between a stupor and a dream, trying to sort out what I knew about Dominic Santos and hoping that it would somehow come together for me. I worried about details that did not matter. I was a man who needed to sleep but who could not shut out the world and so the world flooded me with inconsequential annoyances, nits that needed to be picked, and questions that danced in my head like cartoon words plastered on an IMAX screen.

At some point I convinced myself that I had drunk too much booze and that I should pass out and sleep it off. Whatever I was trying to figure out could wait, primarily because I still did not understand the question.

My last thought before the darkness completely grabbed me was that it had been a long day.

FOUR

IT WAS A good bet that Fermín Santos and Mariele Castilla would visit again, with more questions. And I had to admit that I was as curious as the ill-fated cat.

At nine in the morning I called my office and Rosa answered, right on time, so cheery that I could see her smile over the phone line. I explained that I would be in later, that I had some errands to run.

"You hung over, Louie?"

"I don't get hangovers. Anyway, I didn't drink last night. I just have some things I need to do. Actually, it's for the Santos file. You heard about the riot at the jail?"

I put down my glass of Alka-Seltzer so my secretary wouldn't hear the fizz.

"Pretty much closes that file, doesn't it? Or does the family still need something?"

"That's what I'm working on. I think I should find out what I can about Dominic and the riot. Don't you?"

She waited to answer. I was serious about my question. I wanted her opinion.

"Yeah, I guess so. Mariele Castilla already left a message for you. Said she would call later."

!!!

I started with Danny Frésquez, a man who served proudly and

loyally with the Denver Sheriff's Department and who thought that he owed me a favor because I had represented his no-account brother several times, always with the specter of the brother's addiction threatening to tarnish Danny's law-enforcement career. Danny's gratitude didn't spring from the fact that I managed to mitigate the damage that could have been dumped on the brother, but more that I had kept Danny's name out of the police reports.

I didn't leave my house until close to noon. I found Danny sitting in his back yard with a six-pack and a tape of oldies enjoying a day off in the fashion of any other respectable working man who lived on the North Side. He had finished an extra-long shift because of the riot, hadn't slept, and had concluded that he might has well go with the flow and party until he dropped. I declined his offer of a Bud. In the background, while I explained what I was looking for, Frankie Lymon asked why fools fall in love.

Bleary-eyed and slow-talking, Danny offered, "You have terrible luck, Louie. This could have been a good case for you. The family has money to pay you a nice fee. High profile. You get publicity no matter how it goes. And it had the political twist you like—a 'power to the people' angle, *raza* versus white man's money, all that bullshit." He stalled, then finished without any drama. "Too bad."

"My luck must be better than Dominic's, don't you think?"

"Yeah, sure. But the guy wasn't just in the wrong place at the wrong time, know what I mean? He was right there in the middle of the *chingazos*, throwing down with the hard-core fools. I think he knew what it meant to be in a jailhouse rumble. He sure acted like he did."

"How did the trouble start? You know anything about that?"

"Your man, Santos, and another guy, a real grease ball named Tyler Boudin. They were at each other since the day Boudin got locked up, a day or two after Santos checked in. Those two did *not* like each other from the get. Eventually one of them got himself a shank, somebody gets cut, there's blood on the floor and the walls, and when the other animals get a whiff of it, they freak and tear up the place. Santos got decked with a pipe that split open his skull like a ripe cantaloupe."

"By Boudin?"

"We don't know, Louie. That's on the level. It got so crazy in there, we couldn't see everything that was going on."

"How about the surveillance cameras? Don't the tapes show anything?"

"Yes, some of it. But those assholes started a fire, and then we tear-gassed the unit, and the smoke fucked up everything, including the view from the cameras. I saw Santos and Boudin going at it toe-to-toe, but the smoke blew in and I lost track of them. I got a little busy."

My father was right. The world was on fire.

I liked Danny Frésquez and I believed him. If he said that he didn't know who put out Dominic Santos's lights, that meant that no one in the Sheriff's Department knew.

He continued.

"Personally, I think it was one of the other residents who got behind Santos and clubbed him, not Boudin. One of the Mexican bros. Santos didn't play favorites. He was an equal opportunity creep and he could have been hit with a little brown-on-brown action. He pissed off everybody."

"Including the guards?"

Frésquez's laugh was dry and tight.

"Some of the guards hated his guts. But, if you're thinking that one of the deputies whaled on Santos, that's wrong, Louie. It didn't go down that way. No, Santos got it from one of the prisoners. It doesn't pay to rile the feelings of the inmates. Very few of them can turn the other cheek. Know what I mean?"

"And Boudin?"

"He ended up with a gash across his rib cage. I'm pretty sure Santos gave that to him."

"What's the sheet look like for Boudin? I don't know this guy, do I?"

"He wouldn't come to you, Louie. White power, Aryan Nation crap. The Denver PD busted him soaking pseudo-ephedrine."

"He got caught with his hands full of cold tablets? Is that it?" Frésquez looked worried.

"What? The feds pop guys for that stuff all the time. The pills are soaked in water to capture ephedrine, the main juice in methamphetamine. You need licenses to even have it around, at least in the quantities that Boudin did."

"So why didn't the DEA bring him in? You're talking about federal licenses, federal charges. You said it. It's usually the feds, the Drug Enforcement Agency, who pull off these raids."

"It wasn't exactly a raid, Louie. The Denver cops got a tip and they pinched Boudin without much of a fuss. He was the only one around but he *was* caught red-handed. I expect the DEA agents will eventually get in the act. It's on hold now anyway. Boudin's handcuffed to an infirmary bed, cussing out your boy Santos and anyone else who comes around."

I grabbed a bean and beef special and a couple of large Cokes at the Original Chubby's and had my late breakfast in the parking lot, along with several other customers who ate in their cars in the traditional Chubby's manner. While I ate I read the newspaper account of the jailhouse riot. I belched green chile and carbonation all the way to the hospital and Fermín Santos. The hangover that I told Rosa I never suffered eased up a notch.

The old man was in bad shape. Tubes protruded from his body and hooked up to machines with dials. I was acutely aware of the beep-beep-beep of a heart monitor. The scene reminded me of the time my father had been in the same hospital, almost the same room, and I had prayed while he slept. That had been the last time I had prayed.

Santos was awake and recognized me.

"Mr. Móntez. I hoped you would come by. What happened to Dominic? No one will tell me anything. The doctors, nurses, no one! A policeman stuck his ugly head in here early this morning, and even he would not say much. Except that Dominic was dead. That kind of news, he didn't seem to have any trouble telling me. I told him that Matthew Barber killed my son, but he said that was impossible! Of course it was Barber. There's no doubt."

"Don't get yourself worked up again, Mr. Santos. Dominic was killed during a riot at the jail. I'm afraid that Dominic was as much to blame for the riot as anyone else."

"What do you know about what happened to my son?"

I told him everything I had learned from Danny Frésquez and the newspaper. I didn't leave out anything including Danny's opinion that Dominic Santos was a hated man who attracted trouble and who probably had no one but himself to blame for his own death.

When I finished the old man didn't say a word, didn't move, didn't offer any acknowledgment that he had understood what I had said.

I said, "Your check, Mr. Santos. You can have it — "

He cut me off.

"No. Talk to Mariele about that."

A nurse came in and said that I had to leave.

"Goodbye, Mr. Santos. Maybe —"

He grabbed my arm and pulled me closer to him.

He said, "The man who fought with Dominic. You're sure his name was Tyler?"

"Yes. Tyler Boudin. Why?"

"A few months ago, Matthew Barber had a man working for him. A man named Tyler. Ask Mariele about him. Ask Mariele."

The nurse removed Santos's grip from my arm and politely but firmly ushered me out of the old man's room.

There was nothing more I had to do about Dominic Santos or his father or the San Luis Valley water war. I had been hired for one job and that job never made it past the county jail. The prospective client's girlfriend didn't think she had to tell me all of the truth, and the prospective client had died with his brains and blood smeared on a concrete floor. All I had left was the feel of the old man's weak and shaky fingers pressing into my arm, urging something on me that I didn't want. I rubbed my arm but I couldn't rub that feeling away. I wished that I had accepted Danny Frésquez's offer of a beer.

I had one more stop before my office.

Max Macías had been a lawyer when I was playing Cowboys and Indians with my *mocoso* cousins. He should have retired a while back but he kept at it because he was still good at it and his clients wouldn't let him quit. Over the years of my own practice he had shown me the difference between being a lawyer and being a good lawyer—a lesson I still hadn't learned to his satisfaction.

Max owned a building near City Park, on the east side of downtown. The building was a two-story impressive edifice that had once served quite well as a bordello, back in the days when Denver was a bit more honest about its peccadilloes.

Max's always busy office gave off an air of dignified but friendly professionalism and it was no different that day when I walked in hoping to find him with a few spare minutes to talk to his old clerk.

Vases of freshly-cut flowers and plastic impersonators were placed on tables, in corners, and along the wall. The arrangements were mostly made up of roses and lilies. Red, lilac and white splashes of color attempted to soften the hard edges that lawyers bring to any setting, but some of the flowers had withered.

Three different students sat at computers in the library, dozens of manila folders spread around them like fans. Law students loved to clerk for him because he wasn't shy about using them in real, practical ways: interviewing clients, drafting documents, writing briefs, helping him in the courtroom. They didn't merely serve as research robots. Max would have let them argue cases in court if he could have talked the judges into going along with the idea.

In the waiting room, an elderly woman munched on her fingertips while she tried to control a young girl who insisted on pulling apart the magazines that had been stacked on a squat table.

A dark-haired woman in a multi-colored dress and large, shiny earrings sat behind a desk in a first floor office. I assumed she was the latest in a long line of associates who worked with Max for a year or two then moved on to their own practices where they usually did well, especially with all the referrals that Max sent them.

The receptionist was somebody I did know—Max's youngest daughter, the only one of his four children who was not a lawyer but, then, she hadn't graduated from college yet.

"Well, Mr. Móntez. It's been a while since we've seen you around here. Dad will be happy that you dropped by."

"Hello, Carmen. Please, don't call me Mr. Móntez. I feel old enough already. I remember when you . . ."

She laughed and interrupted me before I could get started on moldy stories about when she ran around the office wearing only a diaper and a ribbon in her hair.

"Oh no, don't go there, please! I'll ring Dad for you. He's upstairs, in the study. Go on up." Then she added, "Louie." She laughed again.

The study had been the master bedroom for Madame Lee, a previous owner who must have made more money in that room in one year than I would make in my entire career. Max had converted the room and adjoining bathroom into a personal library and den where he could relax amidst the comfort of soft, overstuffed chairs and the sweet smoke of an occasional cigar that he sneaked upstairs. Every inch of wall space was taken up with books: biographies, a few novels, and rows and rows of legal treatises on every conceivable legal subject. The place had a bookshelf music system and a small color television set, but I never knew Max to disturb the quiet of the upper room with anything other than his own snoring.

He met me as I finished the flight of stairs. Max seemed shorter than I remembered, and I had always remembered him as short anyway. His trademark bushy Zapata mustache and full head of silver hair accented garish suspenders over dark shirts. It was an image he had carefully cultivated and preserved. But Max had aged. His grip was less firm, his step a bit slower, and when he sat down he visibly winced.

"Goddamn, Luis. It's been too long since we've seen each other. How the hell are you? How's the practice? How are your boys?"

Max wanted to know it all and I told him. We talked for

several minutes, filling in the details of our lives that can be important at times like that. The conversation slowed down when I asked him how his health was holding up.

He shook his head.

"Damn if I know, Luis. Damn doctors can't give a man a straight answer. One week I got high blood pressure, the next they're poking around my prostate, and then they want to be sure that my diabetes isn't acting up. I feel great, if you want to know the truth."

His eyes betrayed that he was lying about how he felt, and I considered that his prerogative.

"Glad to hear that, Max. When you going to settle down so you and Cora can enjoy your hard-earned money?"

He smiled like I had said something that was exactly what he had been thinking. Max's smile was good at creating that illusion.

"I've been going over that same point with my wife and kids. I think this year is the one, Luis. Turn over what's left of my practice to Isabella, you might have seen her downstairs? She's good Luis, one of the best that's ever worked here. She's bright, hard-working, and goddamn terrific in court. She's the one who's kept this law office open. Maybe Max, Jr., will come in with her. He's been at the City Attorney's office long enough and wants to set up a practice. The timing is right for everyone."

He nodded and smiled. He looked pleased with the prospect of someone else taking the business, and that's when I knew that Max was very sick.

He shrugged and shook his head.

"I'm sure you didn't come by to hear an old man talking about retiring. What can I do for you, Luis?"

"I do need some information, Max, and I think you can help."

"Anything, son. You know that. You're part of the damn family."

One thing his opponents would say about Max—he was always polite. I would add disingenuous. I had never felt like part of his family. For one thing I didn't have the legal smarts that seemed to run in the Macías clan like divorces ran in mine.

For another, although he had taught me and patiently shown me the way a Mexican-American attorney should handle himself in the white man's courtrooms, he hadn't always appreciated what he called my "radical proclivities" or the more crude aspects of my business, and had shied away when I had landed in trouble with the bar association. I hadn't blamed him for that. I had acted like a *pendejo* for many years, a man who stumbled over more than his expected share of muck, and Max had not been the only old friend who had turned his back on me.

I got to the point for my visit. "Am I right in remembering that you were part of the legal team that represented those folks in the San Luis Valley when they took on the Sangre de Cristo Water Company?"

"Are you involved with that, Luis?"

He slapped his thigh.

"Of course! The fire and that man killed in the jail last night. That damn Fermín wants you to do something about it. Of course!"

"I was going to defend Dominic Santos on the charges from the fire. That's my involvement."

"Sure, sure. I see. But now that Dominic's dead —?"

"The father wants me to tie up any loose threads. You know how he is."

Max's eyes turned thoughtful. Once again he was the master giving invaluable advice to the apprentice. "Watch out for that man, Luis. Fermín Santos is a tough old sonofabitch. We went around and around for thirty years while the cases worked their way through the system. Water court, federal court. We even filed some damn state court claims, but they got tossed out pretty quickly. That man was so closed-minded! There was no way to work with him. It had to be his way or *nada*, nothing. Eventually, I quit dealing with him and left that to the other lawyers on the team. No love lost between us, that's for damn sure!"

"What was his claim? Why did he think he was entitled to the water rights?"

"His case had merit, Luis. That was the bad part of the way it turned out." He was excited, back in the game and happy for the chance. "The Santos family had been on that land since before the Mexican government issued land grants. The Santos land was part of the Espinoza grant in 1843 and their claim should have been protected by the Treaty of Guadalupe Hidalgo in 1848. Can you imagine constructing a case based on the property law of Spain, Mexico and the U.S. back in the Nineteenth Century? The problem is that somewhere over the years, bits and pieces of the land, and the water rights, were sold off by different family members. When the U.S. Congress ordered a survey in 1854, to clear up the land grants, none of the water rights were included in the Santos holdings. There's no doubt he owns the land. The surveyor general's report confirms that. But there's also no doubt, now, that the water and the water rights belong to the water company. Over the years they bought up all the small holdings, put all the rights into one big package. At the innumerable hearings for that damn case all we could show to substantiate the Santos claim were ancient letters from one Santos to another, mentioning the water and grazing rights. But the lawyers for the water company had deeds of sale, and that damned Congressional survey that was confirmed by an act of Congress in 1860. Nothing we could do about that. It was worth a try, but now it should be over. Unfortunately, it will never be over for Fermín Santos."

A touch of regret tinged the end of his summary.

I tried to sound upbeat. "Sounds like a hell of a case, Max."

He nodded. "Damn right. Hell of a case."

"How about Dominic? How active was he in the legal squabble? How big of a role did he play?"

Max rubbed his chin with brown, pudgy fingers.

"To tell the truth, for many years he wasn't even around. There were other children—two others, actually. Dominic's older brother and sister. But the case, and their father, wore them out. They left the valley and moved on, the boy to Albuquerque and the girl to Los Angeles. I don't think they even talk with the old man. Ah, it's been so many damn years!"

"Even before I came to work for you."

"That's right! The case started when Fermín was a young man. Hell, *I* was young back then. You asked about Dominic. I don't remember even hearing about Dominic until he was arrested in New Mexico and his father asked me for advice about the charges. But by then, we had been in the case for years, Luis. After he was released from prison he showed up at case meetings and in the courtroom. There was a group of valley people who were the actual plaintiffs, but everyone knew Fermín was the man calling the shots. Dominic's presence didn't change any of that. In fact, he got in the way more than once. He would disrupt meetings by saying that we were all wasting time and that the lawyers were only in it for their fees. ¡*Cabrón*! The lawyers worked on that case for years without getting one dime. We all did it because we thought it was a cause that was right. And when Dominic started saying that crap, well, some of the lawyers pulled out. They wouldn't put up with it."

"What was his solution? How did he think the case should be litigated?"

"Oh, for him it was to hell with the courts and the lawyers. You know how some of these kids are. He wanted to confront the people who ran the water company. He wanted a fight, Luis. It wasn't a matter of business or legal rights or any of that. It was personal. His family against the water company, and the last man standing gets it all. I heard from some of the others in the group that he talked about shooting it out with Matthew Barber. Can you imagine? Same old hot-headed thinking that never got us anything, right Luis?" It was obvious that Max was digging at me. It was something he had done before and, just as I had done before, I ignored the dig. As far as I was concerned, Max was dealing in my forgotten history.

"Max, did you ever see Mariele Castilla at the meetings?"

He rubbed his chin again. His eyes brightened for a minute, then faded.

"Yes, the woman. But I don't know much about her. She was just around. But the damn memory is shot, Luis. So, who knows?"

He smiled.

"How about a man named Tyler? Worked for Matthew Barber? Ever run into him?"

The smile flattened into a tight-lipped line.

"There was a man with that name. Big man, ugly man. Tattoos on his arms. Seemed out of place in the valley."

"He worked for Barber?"

"U-mmm. I don't know for sure. I guess he could have. It's possible. But, Luis, the way I remember it, this guy Tyler was a friend or acquaintance of Dominic Santos. I think someone told me that they were in prison together. I could be wrong about all that, Luis. Sorry, but I think I'm retiring at the right time."

"That's okay Max. We can do only so much. Thanks for your time. I'll quit interrupting your day and let you get on with your work. Tell everyone hello for me: Max, Jr. and Erlinda and John and Cora, of course. And you take care of yourself, Max. Enjoy that retirement."

"Hell yes, Luis. You betcha. I'm going to enjoy it for as long as I can. And Luis, you be careful, son. I worry about you. I've always worried about you. You're one of a kind. Remember that." The smile returned for a second. He leaned back in his chair, closed his eyes and grimaced as he took a deep breath.

FIVE

ROSA WORE A teal smock dotted with pink and yellow slashes of color. She was not embarrassed by her body, which Harry López had insensitively described as "large," and she framed it with colorful clothes that reflected her Latina pride. I was happy that she showed up each morning ready for work. I accepted as an extra perk the fact that her clothes livened up my drab office.

She handed me yellow slips of paper that contained her small, precise handwriting.

"A dozen messages altogether, three from Mariele Castilla. Sounds like she's in a bad way. Wants you to call her at the number she left *right away*. How's the hangover?"

I wrinkled my face hoping that she understood that to mean "what are you talking about, girl?"

I sauntered to the back of the building where I had set up my office. I heard the musical notes of the main office phone and Rosa say, "Móntez Law Office. Can I help you?" Rosa had programmed the phone chimes to reflect her outgoing personality rather than her boss's well-known sourness.

As I sat at my desk, my own phone rang.

Rosa said, "It's that Castilla woman again. You want it?"

"Sure."

The phone rang again and I answered it almost immediately.

I expressed my condolences about Dominic and said that if there was anything I could do, she just had to ask.

She didn't waste any time. "There is something that we need help with. Actually, it's not me, it's Fermín. I saw him just a few minutes ago. I'm still here at the hospital. He's getting crazy about this. Crazier, I mean. He's talking wild, that's he going to make somebody suffer for Dominic's death. He said that he knows Matthew Barber had something to do with it. I tried to reason with him, told him he was letting his grief take control. But he won't listen to me. He said that somehow it was Barber's fault that Dominic was in jail. And that Barber probably had him killed. He's going to do something stupid. Can you help?"

Her words had taken me by surprise. An old man, weakened by illness? How could he harm anyone? Let him vent, I thought. Better to spit it out than keep it bottled up.

"I'll talk with him, if you think that will do any good. But aren't you overreacting? What can he do to Barber from his hospital bed?"

"He's Fermín Santos. He thinks he can do anything he wants! I'm afraid he's going to hurt somebody, or get himself hurt. Dominic inherited many things from his father including the old man's anger."

And why is this my problem, I thought.

"He said he had contacted one of Dominic's old friends. He said that Barber had better watch his back. Someone's going to hurt Matthew Barber. Maybe kill him. What can we do?"

"You should go to the police, that's what. If Santos hired someone to kill Barber, you have to let the authorities know so that they can stop it, and they can warn Barber. It's seems pretty clear to me." I couldn't believe the conversation. The respected but stubborn old man who expected revenge for the death of his worthless son had been accused by his pseudo daughter-in-law of hiring a hit man.

"I'm not going to the police! I'm talking about Dominic's father! Hasn't he been through enough? He's lost everything he's worked for, and now the one son who was still on good terms with him is dead. But I don't want anyone else to get hurt, including Fermín. Maybe *you* can warn Barber?"

"So Barber can report this mess to the police? Not only will that get Santos arrested, it means you get picked up, too. Conspiracy, aiding and abetting. Cops don't overlook those kinds of details, especially since there's already been one attempt on Barber's life."

She thought about what I had said. Then, surprisingly, she agreed. "Of course. I'm not thinking right. That's why I need your help. We can't tell Barber. We have to find the man Fermín hired. We can stop him. I've got some money. It shouldn't be that difficult to pay him enough to leave Barber alone, to leave the state if necessary."

"That's not the kind of work I do. I accepted your retainer to represent Dominic in a criminal case, not chase around the state for a hired killer. I'll return the check. I haven't earned it. Use the money to hire someone who can give you what you want. Not that I think you should go through with your crazy idea, but you need a private investigator, someone like that."

She sighed.

"You can keep the money, Luis. Fermín insists. When we came to you for help, we knew what we were getting. Harry López made the recommendation, but Fermín had you checked out. He talked to some of the lawyers who worked on his water rights cases. He talked to people in the valley who knew about you from some of the work you've done down there. We had a good picture of you before we met you, Luis. We knew what we were getting and we thought you were the right man. I still think you are the right man to help me now. I can trust you."

"How the hell do you know that? What makes you think I'm not going to the cops myself? Why should I do anything for any of you? It's wrong, even dangerous. This guy hired by Santos, why would he listen to us? Why would he let us go on our way after he knows that we know what he agreed to do for Santos? No, this is all insanity."

She did not respond and I assumed that she was considering what I had said. I knew I wasn't getting involved in her scheme and I didn't want to know any more about Santos and his dead son. What I had already found out had convinced me that the family was bad news. Nice people don't get beat to death in county jail riots, and nice people don't make calls from their sick beds to hired killers, and nice people don't hide murder conspiracies from the police.

"Okay, Luis." She sounded beaten, resigned. "Maybe you're right. Like I said, I'm not thinking clearly. I just know that Fermín is making a big mistake and I was trying to help him without getting him into any more trouble. But, I guess you're right."

More sighs came across the phone line loud and clear.

Maybe I owed her something, I thought. The ten thousand dollar check in the wallet in my coat pocket pressed against my heart like a straitjacket. I rationalized what I should do. She had reached out for help and all I had given her was a standard lawyer rap. Take it easy, Móntez. Where's your sympathy?

"Maybe we can do something. Let me think about it. Let's meet later. We can talk. I've got some more questions anyway. But now, I have to get back to work."

"Yes, I'd like that." Another sigh, but one of relief. "I have to finish up with all the details for Dominic and Fermín insists on leaving the hospital, so I have to take care of that, too. He's going to spend the night at Nick Medina's house, an old friend. That's where we both were going to stay, before he got sick. But, now, it's better that I give him some time with his friend. I'll stay at the Sagebrush, out by the Tech Center. Do you know it?"

"I know where it is. You want to meet there?"

"Around eight, okay? I should have everything taken care of by then. Maybe we can have some dinner?"

I never learn, I thought.

"Okay. Around eight at the Sagebrush."

⋮

I did get some work accomplished and Rosa was quite pleased with my burst of energy. That's what my professional life was all about — keeping my secretary happy.

I drafted motions, made phone calls, set appointments with new clients, and reviewed a few files I had neglected for several days. The humdrum of the work reinforced the nagging idea that I had played with for several months. My visit with Max

Macías had almost cinched my desire to chuck it all, to get out of the lawyer racket and quit once and for all the career that had turned into a job.

Hell, I was one of the lawyers in town who had worked for Max when Max was still fresh, still a fairly new act in the Hispanic Bar Association gallery of stars. And that made me close to over-the-hill. After almost thirty years, I was entitled to something else, wasn't I? I had gone through my highs and lows, the good and bad and real ugly. But the tough parts were over. I didn't sweat the bankruptcy of my business anymore, at least for most of the year, and no one brought up unseemly reminders about my own incarceration, the temporary suspension of my license to practice law, or the nasty headlines involving women with guns and men with bad attitudes. No, now I was just Luis Móntez, Esq. I was looked at as one more older attorney running out the string, keeping it together until I could afford to ride off into the attorney sunset. Not in the same style as Max, of course, but then Max and I had never shared styles.

My uptight attitude, that nagging strain that gave me headaches, coupled with a lot more drinking—I rationalized were signs that I was tired, beat-up and wrung-out, and closing shop sounded more and more like a good idea. Telling Rosa—that was a downside. She would preach and cajole and threaten and not simply because she liked her job. She thought we did good work together and she didn't want that to stop.

Got to do what I got to do, Rosa.

![ornamental divider]

I stayed at my office until six, the time when I thought I had the best chance of finding Harry López. The guy was worse than a vampire. Daylight scared him, apparently, because the times were few that I could recall seeing him before the sun went down, even when I worked on his cases, except for court appearances that he couldn't shake. Then he looked bleak—pale, wan, drained, like he did on the day he found me at the court library.

I made it over to the Billiards Centre, a fancy name for what

43

we used to call a pool hall. The Centre thrived on Tennyson not far from Thirty-Eighth Avenue with a clientele of eightball hustlers, college neophytes, and a few very serious players who were actually into the science of the game of billiards. Harry liked to start his day there, in the shank of the evening, before he went on to bigger and more lucrative games of chance.

He saw me as soon as I walked in the door. The place was one large room with four rows of pool tables and nothing obstructed any view. Harry ignored my entrance and didn't acknowledge me when I stood next to him as he tried to line up a shot. He was playing against a young man with a nervous habit of constantly rubbing chalk on his stick. Harry didn't give him many chances to use his stick so the chalk was rather irrelevant, I thought.

"Harry, I need to talk with you."

He shot and scratched the eight ball.

"Sonofabitch!"

He threw his stick on the table and angrily dropped a dollar bill next to it.

Harry finally looked at me.

"Look what you made me do. Don't you know better than to talk to a man when he's shooting? Come on, Louie, you owe me a buck for that."

"Don't start on who owes who again. You can't win that argument, Harry."

He moved away from the college kid who had sprouted a huge, disrespectful victor's grin. I followed Harry to a pair of chairs in the back of the room, against the wall, ostensibly for spectators. The chairs were all the privacy we were going to find in that place.

He glanced nervously at his watch then demanded, "What is it? I don't have a lot of time. I have an appointment in about twenty minutes. Across town. Business."

"This won't take long. Tell me all you know about Castilla and Santos. You heard what happened?"

"Yeah. Too bad. I didn't know Dominic all that well, but getting put down in county can't be a pleasant way to go. Guess your case is over, huh?"

"You'd think. But they want me to stay involved, and I can't exactly see why. And now Mariele wants me to chase down some guy she thinks the old man hired to get some revenge. What the hell did you get me mixed up in?"

"Whoa, Louie." He squeezed his hands together as though he knew how to pray. "It wasn't me, bud. They came to me, wanted a lawyer. They had some names but you were high on the list and I gave you a good reference. So you got the retainer. You did get some money from them, didn't you?"

I didn't want to bring Harry into my business affairs. I had already pushed all the limits of intimacy with him that I could bear.

I said, "The old man had his heart attack or whatever it was before we talked about all the details. And now the client's dead. I don't think I'm going to make much money from your referral, Harry. So, I ask again, what do you know about these people?"

I wanted to grab his neck and squeeze the words out of him but I held myself in check and let him ramble on about Mariele and Fermín in his own labored, slow way.

The Santos family were the well-to-do branch of his mother's side of the family. Santos was not a warm and fuzzy uncle but Harry tried to keep on the old man's good side.

"That *viejo* has some bucks. Never know what might drift down my way, know I'm saying? So I did them the favor of introducing you to them. What's the harm in that? I'd thought you would welcome the job. Guess I was wrong."

"No, Harry, it's not that. It just got weird real quick. They really do things like what Mariele is telling me the old man wants to do?"

He cleared his throat and turned up the sides of his mouth as if he were chewing on a thought. Empty calories.

Finally he said, "That's hard for me to believe, to tell you the truth. The old man's not that way. But this Mariele. She's another story. She could probably talk the old man into something stupid. And she knows some people. Guys I wouldn't want to get on the wrong side of, I'll admit that. But the old man thinks she's the best thing since *huevos rancheros*. Supposedly did wonders for Dominic—we see how far that went, hey? Anyway, if you want my advice, I think it's a good chance for you to make some large bread. Like I said, the old man's loaded, for an old Mexican guy, that is, and if it was me I'd burn up those billable hours for him. Take a little trip down to the valley, talk to a few people, get paid for your time. What you got to lose, dog?"

It was easy for Harry. Bread, money, billable hours. What else did I need? He had steered some action my way and I looked ungrateful. Milk it, Harry was saying. Get some of that green stuff from the uncle. He said it and he was serious about it. The possibility that I might balk, that I might have some qualms about the deal didn't sit right with Harry. Maybe he could ignore those "guys" Mariele knew, but I wasn't sure I could.

I let Harry get back to his work. He had "an appointment," a "business thing," and the less I knew about it the cleaner I would feel. About that, I was positive.

SIX

I DROVE SOUTH through clogged traffic on the always-under-construction interstate to the Arapahoe exit and steered the car east until I saw the bright green **SAGEBRUSH INN** sign. The more I moved away from the north side of town, the thicker the smoke from the fires in the foothills. Details were difficult to make out, but the sign flashed at me like a lighthouse on the coast.

The place was nice, not part of a chain, but it acted like the Ramada Inn's younger sister. The clean, spacious lobby had southwestern flavor generously supplied by management—Indian blankets on the walls, Saltillo tile for the floor, and on turquoise-colored shelves, bronze sculptures of wild horses and buffalo. A plaster sleeping Mexican with a giant plaster sombrero squatted against a plaster saguaro. I would never rent a room at the Sagebrush.

The so-called inn had an indoor swimming pool, a bar and a restaurant. Mariele Castilla waited for me in the bar.

She had changed from her country gear into a white sleeveless dress with embroidered flowers around the neckline. The flowers reminded me of Max Macías's office. The silver and turquoise barrette still held her hair but she had added a bit of makeup around her eyes and on her lips. I was appropriately impressed and a little flattered.

She had ordered a rum and Coke and when it arrived I

asked for a beer. We helped ourselves to nachos while we talked. The subject of dinner did not come up.

Five minutes into the nachos, I asked, "Does the name Tyler Boudin mean anything to you?"

She quickly nodded her head.

"Of course. The man who was in the fight with Dominic. The police told me about him. They're questioning him about his past connections to Dominic. He might have killed Dominic. He lived in the valley last year. Worked for Barber for a month or two. That's probably why the two of them fought in the jail. Dominic hated anything or anyone who had ties to Barber."

"Did Dominic know Boudin before last year? In prison?"

She said nothing for a few seconds.

"I don't think so, Luis. Dominic would have mentioned that to me. Anyway, Tyler Boudin was not the kind of person Dominic would associate with. Boudin gave me the creeps. The way he looked at women, the way he talked about Mexicans and Blacks."

"And the last time you or Dominic saw this guy Boudin was last year? Not since then?"

"He left the valley and we all said good riddance. It was just Dominic's bad luck that he was in jail at the same time."

"Yeah. Bad luck."

She scooped salsa on a chip and ate. Red lines cracked the white of her eyes.

When she finished chewing, she said, "I guess you won't be going to the valley with us? We're leaving tomorrow. Fermín insists. He wants to get back to his own doctor anyway."

"I'm not planning to leave the city. Maybe you two should wait a few days. Maybe the *viejo*'s mind can be changed."

She sipped her drink.

"I'm certainly going to try. But we do have to get back. I have to set up Dominic's funeral. I arranged for him to be taken down there. The police said they would be done with him, with the body and everything. So I guess that's all we need to do here. We don't belong in the city. Isn't it obvious?"

I slipped the envelope with the check from my pocket and

pushed it across the table to her. She hardly glanced at it before she shoved it in her purse.

I watched the woman eat tortilla chips and drink dark rum and play with a loose strand of her hair. I ignored the scars on her wrists. I listened to her talk about her dead boyfriend, about how easily he could get agitated, about his temper, but also about his loyalty to his father and his ambitions to turn the Santos ranch into something more, to build on what his father had started. She told me how Dominic had tried to repair the relationships with his brother and sister, but they had rebuffed him. She said that they had talked about marriage, maybe one of these days. She said she hadn't meant to drag me into her personal life and that she didn't blame me for not wanting to get more involved. Then she started crying.

She excused herself and ran off. I attracted the attention of the waitress and paid the bill and then wasted five more minutes arguing with the desk clerk until he finally gave me her room number.

I knocked and waited for a few heartbeats. She opened the door and stepped back in the room. I moved forward, grabbed her in my arms and kissed her. She kissed me back and hugged me so tight that I could feel the embroidered flowers of her dress pressed against my shirt. She pulled the barrette from her hair.

I kicked the door shut and she led me to the bed.

⁞

At four in the morning I lay next to her, wide awake. The sex had been frenzied, rough. She had told me what she wanted and let me know when it was not enough. My skin was pinched and bitten and scratched, hers even more so. She used words that at another time would have made me wince. We made love in a sweat-drenched fury that left me saddened and lonely. When we finished she cried again and broke down. I tried to comfort her as she ridiculed and condemned herself for what she had done. She finally fell asleep but there was no such relief for me. No one comforted me, no one talked me out of my own ridicule and condemnation.

Part Two
The Big Man and The Bartender

SEVEN

WE MADE EXCUSES for one another. Mariele had to use a great deal of imagination to come up with any for me that sounded halfway logical.

The one thing she didn't waver on was her belief that we had to stop Fermín Santos from making the biggest mistake of his life. While we drank coffee in Styrofoam cups from the complimentary pot in the lobby she again asked for my assistance.

"Luis, I can't do this alone. If you help me find the man Fermín hired, we can stop him and we can put an end to the fighting and anger that's taken over Fermín's life. He's an old man. He doesn't care about the consequences. He doesn't think he has much time left anyway. You know it's wrong and you know that we can probably do something before it's too late."

The motel room was stuffy and disheveled. No one had made the bed and the evidence of our sexual encounter was spread around us as we talked. I had showered but my skin was coated with a grimy layer of regret.

I told her, "It could already be too late. We don't know what Fermín's guy intends to do, or when."

She disagreed.

"No, we have some time. Fermín won't let anything happen to Barber before Dominic's funeral. He's that way. And he knows that the police will be watching Barber and Barber's ranch, and the water company office. So, things will have to cool down a bit. Maybe two weeks, maybe a month. We've got time, Luis."

From the minute that I had let her take my hand and lead me to her bed I had lost the argument. As I finished off the weak coffee I agreed to join her in the valley as soon as I could get away, and that I would talk with Mr. Santos. It wasn't as much as she wanted me to say but it was enough and we both knew that when the time came I would help her in any way she wanted. She took the coffee from my hand and set it down, then she stepped in my arms and kissed me. Our bargain was sealed.

I pulled away and said, "I've got to go. I wasn't planning to spend last night here and I have a lot to do. I'll let you know when I leave Denver. Don't try to find the man Santos hired until I get there. Talk to the *viejo*. Maybe you can change his mind."

She stood, walked to the corner of her room where her purse sat and took out the envelope with the check. I accepted it. I was working for her and the old man again. I guess I had started during the night.

Then I left. My exit was crass and obvious but she didn't seem to mind. I wasn't surprised by the effect the one-night stand had on me. Very little about myself surprised me and years before I had quit trying to understand my more base motivations. During the long night Mariele had described what we did as a sympathy fuck. The sympathy ran both ways in the bed that night.

I had to get away and somewhere I had picked up an obligation to the Santos family, or at least to Dominic Santos's wife, or girlfriend, or whatever the hell she was. While driving back to central Denver I told myself that I was all right, that I was doing something good, that I was trying to prevent hate, revenge, murder. I would earn that ten grand. I would do my best to convince the old man that he had to let go and move on. I must have signed up for the job because I was so good at it. Letting go and moving on, that is.

:::

"I'll be out of the office for at least a week. I'm taking that vacation you think I need. My court calendar's clear. Cancel the appointments for the next week, then take the time off yourself."

Rosa nodded, giving the impression that I had asked for her permission.

"Good for you, Luis. Some clients won't be happy with you, especially Montoya and the Jiménez family, but they can wait. I'll take care of everything else. Where will you be in case I need to contact you?"

"South. As far south as I can get in a week. I'll be at Dominic Santos's funeral, whenever it happens, so you can reach me for a few days through my nephew, Michael Torres. He's in my Rolodex."

Her eyes peered at me over the rim of her tinted glasses.

"You're going to the funeral? God, that woman must have made *quite* an impression."

"Think what you want, gutter-mind. I'm still working for the family. They want me to go through the appellate decision from the Tenth Circuit, make sure there isn't some grounds for a rehearing, maybe petition the Supreme Court. How would you like to get in on that, Rosa? You and me to Washington, D.C."

It was almost the truth but I could see that she wasn't buying any of it. She slowly shook her head and clicked her teeth.

I handed the check to Rosa, tried to make a big presentation out of the fact that I had a new retainer. I said, "Make sure that gets in the account today." She stuck the check in her desk drawer.

She asked, "What did that woman do to you? *Pobrecito*, Luis. You're such a guy sometimes."

"What the hell is that supposed to mean?"

"Nothing, Luis. Nothing at all."

!!!

Danny Frésquez called me at my house. I was in the middle of packing for the trip but it had been slow because I kept arguing with myself about leaving at all.

"I tried your office but all I got was a message that you're closed for a week. Vacation, huh?"

"You could say that. What's up?"

"It's probably nothing. I just thought you would want to know, since it sounded like you were working on an important case. That guy, Tyler Boudin, from the jail? The one who tangled with your boy Santos?"

"Yeah. What about him?"

"It's strange. He was recuperating from his wound, I thought. Next thing I hear, the charges are dismissed by some idiot judge and Boudin walks away. Doesn't even face anything over the riot. Some of the deputies are really pissed about that. That kind of crap happens, but not to guys like Boudin. At least I thought not to guys like Boudin."

The news that Tyler Boudin was on the street bothered me and not just because he had something to do with the death of my potential client. It wasn't right.

I asked, "What do you make of it?"

"One of two things. Guys with a lot of money and very good lawyers and maybe it's their first offense get this kind of walk. Or, a snitch. Some cop who needs Boudin on something else pulls his ticket and he skates."

"You think Boudin is a snitch?"

"What do you think, Louie? Boudin didn't have any money, he didn't have a lawyer, and this definitely was not his first offense."

"Damn. Boudin's out now? Anyone know where?"

"I wouldn't have a clue about that. I'll see you around. Just thought you would want to know."

I made a phone call I didn't want to make, then I drove downtown. I parked in the lot across the street from the public library, jaywalked Thirteenth, and bought a soda from a hairy hot dog salesman manning a battered but busy sidewalk cart. I continued on the pedestrian walk between the Art Museum and the library, past a giant obscure metal sculpture, and ended up in the amphitheater in Civic Center Park, a few blocks from where I had held Harry López's hand only a few days before. While I waited in the shade of a Greek column, I drank my soda.

Two women jogged through the park and their course brought them to within a few feet of where I sat.

The brunette said, "The basement has really ugly paneling on the walls that we have to get rid of. I hope Walter gets on it soon, but he's so useless around the house."

The blonde responded in grunts from her hard breathing in the sticky heat. "I have . . . a name . . . for you . . . Mexican . . . but cute . . ."

They ran out of my eavesdropping range.

A clean-cut looking woman in a blue suit made her way in my general direction over the bright green of the park grass and against the dirty gray of the park's architecture. She saw me and frowned when she realized she would have to climb steps.

I could have talked with Rolanda Alvarez over the telephone but then she could have avoided my questions and put me on hold and even hung up in my face. Person-to-person had to be better to pry information from the assistant DA, more so because as far as she knew she had no real reason to give me any.

"Luis Móntez. To what do I owe this unexpected pleasure? And make it quick. It's hot out here. Why can't you meet in an office, like any other defense attorney? I assume this is about one of your cases? I don't remember anything I've got with you on the other side."

"Nice to see you, too, Rolanda. Have a seat. Take a load off. Enjoy the fresh air, the joggers running around in gym shorts and sport bras. And why does this have to be about a case? Can't I chew the fat with my ex-wife's sister just to catch up on the latest? How is Gloria, by the way?"

She laughed but it was obvious she didn't find anything funny about my conversation.

"What do you want?" She had always been direct, professional. She was an excellent prosecutor.

"I want to know about a dirt bag named Tyler Boudin."

She stared at me as though I was sitting on a pile of dog waste and she didn't know how to tell me.

She wasn't going to answer me, so I gave her a few details.

"I'll pretend that right now you don't know what I'm talking about, and that I need to fill you in, and then you will have to check on some things, and then you will have to get back to me. Let's just say that's the way it will be, okay?"

"God, you got some nerve. What is this?"

"Call it what you want, Rolanda."

"And why should I do anything for you? It's not like I owe you any favors. I give you a break on a case now-and-then for old times' sake, but that's it. You screwed up a good marriage with Gloria. You got some fine boys that you never see. You've wasted your education, you can't . . ."

"Shut up, Rolanda."

She lost her professional decorum. "You asshole! See you around the courthouse, Móntez."

She whirled to retrace her steps. I followed her and spoke to her well-tailored back.

"Rolanda, take it easy. You're going to help me. If for nothing else, if not because of our past family relationship, which should be enough by the way, then do it because I just happen to know who helps you relieve the tension before trial, late at night, when you should be home. I just happen to know about a cute number who works in your office. A secretary who's good at dictation, I hear, and famous for her short skirts and sexy dance steps."

I let that sink in.

"Did I ask about Dennis, Rolanda? How's he doing, by the way? And your kids?"

I've been around too long, I thought. I know too much about too many people. *Son los años*, in more ways than one.

!!!

I WAITED AT my house for Rolanda's information. A few hours after our meeting she called and gave me what she had learned. She wasn't a lady about it but she didn't hurt my feelings. She *had* to get upset with me, even throw a few aspersions at my poor dead mother and my IQ. She was an assistant district attorney, for crying out loud, forced to dig into a load of dirty laundry. I was a defense attorney messing in something that I had no real good reason to be in, and I had forced her into it and who knows what that might cost her in the future? But for now, she was my pal, my buddy, even if she did think I was a *pinche cabrón* of the highest order.

I pulled out of the city just in time to hit the evening rush hour traffic. From Speer Boulevard to the Happy Canyon exit took me more than an hour, and it was bumper-to-bumper, rage-to-rage all the way. I got flipped off three times. A woman behind the wheel of an enormous SUV nudged my rear bumper after I had squirmed into a space in front of her in the parking lot that should have been a southbound lane.

I didn't let it bother me. I had my radio on as loud as my ears could stand it and the jazz station obliged me with 1920s Louis Armstrong, 1990s Fathead Newman, and timeless Sarah Vaughn. I could have been on a vacation, like Danny Frésquez thought, and I wasn't going to let a few thousand careless, stupid and angry commuters ruin it.

I drove through a rolling, angry gray cloud near Castle Rock that smothered the sun. The latest brush fire had exploded and a range of forest had vanished in a blaze of hatred and confusion. Starting a forest fire had become the latest method of attracting the attention of a wandering lover.

At Monument Hill the station faded and I clicked on a homemade tape of *cantina* music. I listened to a steady refrain of broken hearts, apologetic lovers, and the general torments, trials and tribulations of male Mexican life. By the time the dormant chimneys of the Pueblo steel mill popped up on the horizon, my eyes were almost crying from the memories and pain that such music stirred up, and my dry throat did cry for relief. Mexican music equaled drinking music, any *safado* knew that, and the Mexican known as Luis Móntez needed a drink and Pueblo was a good town for a drink. Any *safado* also knew that.

I navigated the Central Avenue exit and wandered around the Bessemer neighborhood for several minutes before I focused on the bright blue sign that announced **GORDON'S LOUNGE**—Pueblo's Finest. My brother had lived in Pueblo for a few years and he had told me stories that described Gordon's as a bar with good Mexican hamburgers, a great jukebox, and decent service. He said that it was a typical Pueblo watering hole, which meant that it had a steel town feel, a working class ambience—potato chips with red chile powder, tomato beers and Italian sausage sandwiches with mozzarella, thin, garlicky pickle slices, and green chile strips.

A few tables with bright red-and-white checkered plastic tablecloths took up space near the front, vinyl booths hugged the walls, and a busy, smoky bar stretched from the door to the back exit. The crack of pool games mixed with jokes, laughter, plans and schemes, and the ordinary conversation of ordinary people who understood why the world needed joints like Gordon's. Over the din I barely heard an R&B tune that I couldn't recognize. I eased into a stool at the far end of the bar and ordered food and drink.

My rest stop lasted longer than I had planned. The crowd was in a good mood and it didn't take long for me to feel at home with the easy-going booziness and good-spirited letting off of steam. I fell into a long discourse with Ken and Stella, who used to be married but now saw each other only at the bar, and only twice a week, and they never went home with each other.

"Learned that lesson the hard way," Ken informed me.

Alicia, the bartender, kept me in beer and laughter with her jokes about blondes and lawyers, even though I had heard all the jokes. I theorized that humor ran south in Colorado, from Denver to Pueblo. She said I had a strange way of looking at things.

At one point she asked me where I was from and I gave her my name, the fact that I was a lawyer from Denver, and that I was on my way to the San Luis Valley.

"I like the valley," she offered. "Good to get away when you can. But you must be working on something. Got a case down there?"

"Kind of. I'm a little involved in that water fight you might have read about."

"No, can't say that I have. I got my own problems, don't need to read about other folks'."

A whistle from across the room interrupted our talk.

She hollered so that everyone in the bar could hear her.

"Oh no you didn't! Cut the crap, Benny. Don't you be whistling for me. I ain't your pet dog. Damn guy!"

When I wasn't talking with Ken and Stella I warmed up to the bartender and the more beer she poured the more social I got. The time sped by until I realized that I probably shouldn't have had the last beer. Even with the spicy hamburger lining the walls of my stomach, six draws were too much if a person still had three hours of good driving to do and that person was already thinking about a bed for the night.

I left what I thought was a nice tip for Alicia, said so long to Ken and Stella, and stopped by the restroom on my way out.

The stifling, warm Pueblo night was broken only by dim, fluttering illumination from a street light across Northern Avenue. I couldn't see the man waiting for me near my car. Later, I wondered about that, because he was so big he could have been spotted from Los Angeles.

I pulled on my car door and he pulled on me. He spun me around and punched me in the stomach. I fell to my knees and gagged on Mexican hamburger. He picked me up and held me close.

"What you want with Tyler Boudin?"

The word hadn't taken long to spread, I thought. Quicker than I expected, and that had me in a jam.

I coughed an answer.

"I'm a lawyer. I need to talk to him about a case."

He set me down and I sucked in air.

"Start talking, lawyer."

I needed a minute to catch my breath, then I asked, "How did you know I wanted to talk with you?"

He raised his arm and hit me again, this time in the ribs. I sagged against my car and dropped to the street.

"No questions, Móntez. What do you want with Tyler Boudin?"

I looked up and tried to make out details of the man who was beating me. With the help of the weak streetlight, I could see that he had a beard. Long hair. A dark-colored, maybe black, sleeveless tee-shirt. Shadows marked his arms and I figured the shadows were tattoos.

"I'm working for Fermín Santos. I'm trying to find out for him what happened to his son. He just wants to know, that's all. You were in jail with Dominic. You knew Dominic. What do you know about how he died? What do you know about the fire at Matthew Barber's cabin?"

He stood over me. I made it to my knees.

"I said no questions. What the fuck you want to know all that for? You working for the old man, or the cops? You sound like a cop, Móntez. I'll tell you this. I didn't kill Dominic Santos. Not that it matters to me who greased that greaser. I just ain't taking the rap for that. That's all you're getting from me. Understand?"

I hesitated and he grabbed me again.

"I said, do you understand? You quit asking about me, you forget you ever heard of me. You don't even remember my name. You got it, Pancho?"

Why do certain white guys think calling a Mexican Pancho is an insult?

He raised his arm to hit me again. I thought I might as well try to get what I could while I had the chance. "Boudin, wait. You don't have to hit me. All I want is information. Nothing else. I'm not a cop, not going to the cops. I heard you were a pal of Dominic's. That you knew him from the New Mexico pen. If that's right, then what happened in jail?"

"You must be one bad lawyer because you sure don't understand English. But you fucking wetbacks don't need to understand English, do you? Goddamn Mexicans!"

Then he kicked me and punched my face and hit me in the head and knocked me out. He appeared to enjoy saying the words "Goddamn Mexicans."

EIGHT

LATER I LEARNED that Ken and Stella found me on the pavement and that with Alicia's help they carried me inside where Alicia administered bartender first-aid. Ken and Stella left but Alicia stayed with me, long after she should have locked up and called it a night. When I came to she asked if she should call the cops. Alicia understood that discretion was the better part of street brawls and I told her no, the cops were not necessary.

"Where you staying, Móntez? You need some sleep, rest. I'll drive you there."

"I thought I'd be in the San Luis Valley by now. I don't have a place here. I wasn't expecting this. Take me to a motel. I'll just get a room."

My head spun and the floor buckled and I fell to my knees, again. The loss of consciousness had given me a queasy stomach that had me disoriented and lightheaded. She grabbed me and let me lean against her.

"You better stay at my place. Hope you like dogs."

Alicia traveled in a white El Dorado left over from the Nixon years. The back seat had room for me to stretch out as I tried not to bleed all over the fake leather upholstery. She drove to a dirt road off of Lake Avenue near the south edge of the town.

The small, white frame house with chipped siding sat almost alone on a stretch of space that looked more rural than urban. In the moonlight I saw a chain link fence and a small front yard with a receding patch of dry grass. As I crawled out of the car I heard dogs barking and whimpering and Alicia saying something to the animals. I limped in the house with her help and together we made it to a room where she set up a cot for me to sleep. I remember her wiping my face with a wet, warm cloth.

!!i

Bright, yellow light woke me. Sunshine streamed through a window without curtains. The window framed a blue, cloudless sky, and I had the sensation of floating above the earth.

Unlit candles, dried red and yellow marigolds, and photographs of people who looked familiar, who could have been my cousins, nephews, nieces, brothers or sisters, surrounded *La Virgen de Guadalupe*. The Indian Mother of Jesus smiled, her hands clasped in eternal prayer for all us sinners. Her brown skin gave off a glow that radiated from within. I rubbed my eyes, unable to believe that I had died and gone to heaven.

In another corner of the room a computer at least two generations behind the latest Best Buy specials confirmed that wherever I had landed, it wasn't heaven.

The wide band of pain along my rib cage woke me completely and I remembered Alicia and her dogs and the big man and his massive fists.

I smelled food and coffee.

A large black dog ambled up to me, sniffed my bruised face, looked around to make sure I hadn't taken anything, then left.

Alicia followed the dog into the room.

"Good morning. God, that eye looks bad. We better put something on it, although it's too late. How's the rest of you?"

"I think I'll live."

"Good. Don't want anyone dying back here. Although I already got my Day of the Dead altar ready."

She pointed in the direction of the statue of *La Virgen* resting on a table in a corner of the room.

"Just need your picture to stick up there with the rest of the dead folks. If you die."

She sat on the edge of the cot. She scanned my face, rubbed something off my forehead, and asked me to lift the blanket so she could look at my ribs. A large bruise covering most of my left side surprised both of us and when she touched it I flinched. I realized that someone had removed my shirt, pants, shoes and socks.

She apologized for making me twitch. "Sorry. Maybe we should have a doctor look at that. Something could be broken."

"Yeah, maybe. But I'm not having trouble breathing, so I don't think he cracked anything."

I breathed deeply to prove my point and let out the air with more gusto than I should have. A twinge of pain stopped my act.

She left the room and returned a few minutes later with ice cubes wrapped in a towel. She handed the ice-pack to me and I gingerly rested it on my swollen eye.

She asked, "You want some aspirin?"

"No thanks. I just need a drink.'

She laughed.

"You drink too much. And I should know. Ha! Listen to me. A bartender telling a customer he drinks too much. I'll make you some tea, *hierbabuena*. How's that sound?"

I nodded, not sure about how I was feeling.

She said, "Who was that guy? This was more than a mugging. You told me last night in the car to be careful that no one was following us. Actually, you kind of mumbled it more than said it. What are you into?"

"I wish I knew. You shouldn't be part of it. I'll leave. What if that guy—his name's Tyler Boudin—what if he comes back and decides you helped out the wrong Denver lawyer? I got enough guilt playing on my head. I don't need more because of you."

The bright light of the room exposed details of the woman who had taken me in. Her skin and eyes were brown, and hair somewhere between brunette and auburn accented a strong, intense face.

She squinted at me and I realized I had been staring. I moved the ice pack lower on my face and closed my eyes.

She said, "You're not going anywhere, Móntez, except the hospital. I can call the guys at Redi-Ambulance and they'll be here in five minutes. But other than that, you're not leaving this house. I'm your driver, remember?"

My eyes opened.

"Uh, right. I'll need to get my car. But, I'm serious. This could be trouble for you, trouble you don't want. The beating I took last night was just a warning. If I don't heed it, then—"

"Then the big guy breaks *my* ribs? I don't think so. And face it. You can hardly sit up, forget about driving a car. Unless you're wanted by the police I think you stay here until you can drive."

I shrugged and that made me wince.

She took the ice pack from my hand and rearranged the ice cubes.

"And I checked," she added as she ministered to my battered face. "The police don't want you. At least, the Pueblo cops don't. One good thing about bartending. Meet a lot of interesting people. Ambulance drivers, cops, Denver lawyers."

I grunted and eased back onto my pillow.

She stood and petted a yellow dog that had crawled from under the cot.

"Móntez, there is another thing we can do. We can call a friend, family. Someone in Denver who would come down here for you? That option works for me. The only one that doesn't is the one where you leave here by yourself, today."

There wasn't anyone I could call to come and get me. I wouldn't drag Rosa into this. I might have been overprotective, but I had no right to put her in harm's way. I had already involved the innocent bartender. The self-reproach was building up and I wasn't going to add to it by asking someone else for help. And the truth was, aside from Rosa, I couldn't think of anyone I might have called.

"Well, maybe I have a little breakfast, then we see how I'm doing. What do you think about that?"

"The food's ready when you are. You like *chorizo* and eggs, with a few beans and *papas*? That okay for a Denver lawyer?"

"God, quit calling me that. Luis will do, even Louie. Anything except lawyer. Don't you have to go to work?"

"Sure. Have to be at the bar by six tonight."

A half-hour later I climbed off the cot and made my way to

her kitchen. She prepared a plate of food and stuck it in a microwave for a few minutes. She poured me some coffee and the cup of tea.

The beans, potatoes and Mexican sausage were smothered in the same green chile that had covered my hamburger the night before. In a small, cluttered kitchen, I sat across from the bartender who had become my nurse and I ate one of the best meals of my life.

I talked while I ate. I gave her the short version of the Santos family saga and the valley water war. She listened politely and didn't eat enough food to keep her going for the rest of the day and night.

"You should eat more," I said.

"Not all that hungry. The crazy hours in the bar keep my routines up in the air. I started the night shift only about a week ago. Gordon wasn't sure about a woman handling the place at night. But he's okay with it now. Still, I can't get my body clock adjusted. I don't get real hungry until about ten at night, then I gorge myself on the food at the bar. Whatever's left after the evening rush."

"You make the food?"

"Yeah. Head cook and bottle washer and beer maid. All rolled into one package. By the way, if you're still here tomorrow, you do the cooking. I'm not really this domesticated."

I smiled and kept on eating.

She watched me for a few minutes, then finally asked the questions.

"Why would Tyler Boudin beat you up? If he's out from under the Santos jailhouse killing, then why should he care about you?"

"He found out that I was interested in him and he didn't like it. He must have followed me from Denver, waiting for his chance to warn me off of whatever he thought I was doing."

"How would he know that you had even asked about him?"

"Rolanda Alvarez wasn't very discreet, apparently. Somebody along the line tipped off Boudin."

Through the kitchen's screen door I saw three or four dogs prancing around the back yard. About every ten minutes, they all would start barking in a chorus of dog complaints and commentary.

"That's quite a crew you have out there."

"Yeah, they keep me company, that's for sure. Most of them are strays that have stayed longer than I thought they would. It's a bad habit I have. I can't resist a lost dog."

She didn't say any more about her pets or her penchant for taking in strange dogs, or strange men, I thought to myself. She asked another question.

"Why couldn't Boudin have learned about you from Alvarez? From what you said, your former relation doesn't seem to think much of you."

"You got that right. But, for all her faults, and she's got plenty, she's one of those rare people you might have read about. On the level, a real straight arrow. It runs in that family. My ex-wife was exactly the same. Honest to a fault."

Except about her love affairs, I could have added. Gloria had other traits that Alicia might have found interesting but the timing didn't seem right.

Alicia continued with her questions. "Who do you think it was that clued-in Boudin, if not Alvarez?"

"Rolanda told me that Tyler was released and the charges dropped because the feds, meaning the FBI or the DEA, need him for an important sting operation involving major drug dealers in five different states. Colorado's the center of the operation and apparently Tyler Boudin is on the inside of the operation. He's needed to bring it down. He's more than a snitch. Sounds like an undercover cop. His arrest was a 'mistake.' Even if he was involved in the jailhouse riot, the Denver DA's office didn't think he killed Dominic Santos, or at least they couldn't prove it. Also, I'm sure the thinking was, Santos's death meant one less lowlife to deal with, one less expensive trial, one more file marked closed. Everyone agrees to let Boudin go. Then I start asking questions about him. One of the feds passes on the information about Alvarez's questions, and me, and Tyler gets nervous because I might blow his cover. So he tries to warn me off."

Her jaws had quit working in the middle of a bite of *tortilla*.

"Boudin's a cop? A federal agent?"

"I'm almost sure of it. Either that or a snitch of high priority. Someone jumped through a lot of hoops to get him out of jail. Someone went to a lot of trouble for this man. He's either a very important snitch, or a very deep undercover cop."

"But, how could he . . . ? He hurt you bad. He could have killed you."

Now it was my turn to quit chewing.

"It surprises you that a cop can do this? I've handled way too many police brutality cases. Haven't you ever heard of Rodney King, or maybe Ismael Mena?"

"But, this wasn't anything like what you think of when you hear about a police brutality case. This man ambushed you, beat you up, and left you bleeding and hurt in the parking lot. I can't believe it."

"Maybe you'd just rather not believe it."

She cleared the plates off the table and piled them in the sink. She poured herself another cup of coffee and offered me some. I raised my cup and she filled it. I hadn't touched the tea.

Finally, she said, "Yeah, maybe that's it. I don't want to believe it. I'm not naïve about this stuff. At least I don't think I am. Working in that bar for five years I've seen things that I'd just as soon forget. Including crap from the cops. And, in this town, there's always been trouble between Mexicans and everybody else, including the cops and the Blacks. We just don't talk about it that much. But, you and this guy Boudin. I don't know. You're quite an adventure, Móntez. Quite an adventure."

She returned to her kitchen table and looked in my bruised and reddened eyes.

"And all this just because you want to help the old man? Him and the woman? You get beat up. Just for asking. And I guess now you go on to the valley to finish up what you got yourself into, even if it means you get beat up again? Is that about it?"

Her words made me smile because she had it all summed up in a neat, sarcastic bundle.

Her face flushed with a flash of anger, or hurt.

"What are you smiling about? This sounds serious to me. Serious and dangerous."

"Easy. I know it's serious. I'm the guy with the black eye, remember? It's just that I realized that Tyler's visit probably has nothing to do with anything that I can do for Fermín Santos or Mariele Castilla. I just asked the wrong questions about the wrong man."

"That doesn't strike me as funny. Not in the least."

"I got to see the humor in this thing or I'm going to end up feeling sorry for myself. And that is something you don't want to see."

"What makes you think I haven't seen that already?"

I mumbled, "Why did you say that?"

"I listened to you moan about your life last night for a couple of hours in the bar. Everything from your law practice to your family issues to the lack of a sex life. Don't be surprised. Men reveal all kinds of things to their bartenders. Stuff that they don't tell their wives, shrinks, or drinking buddies."

When I had left Gordon's I had never expected to see her again. I could have told her anything.

"I'm usually not that self-pitying."

She quickly interrupted me.

"Hey, wait. Don't do that. I'm used to it, for one thing. And for another, I'm glad I heard that from you. You told me about being uptight, about hassling a guy named López that you called a 'little pipsqueak' and about how that surprised even you. You went on about being burned out on the lawyer gig. You just got into all of it. I can kind of understand how you could get into this mess with the Santos family, now that I know where your head was. And, although you didn't say it, I certainly got a vibe from you about the Castilla woman. There's something there that's also driving you. But, hey, not my business, and I apologize I went on about it. Maybe we better let you get back to bed. You could probably use more sleep."

"Yeah, sure."

What else could I say?

I shuffled to the back room.

As she filled the sink with water to clean the dishes she said, "Luis Móntez. Yes, sir. Quite an adventure." She hummed a melody that I recognized as a song that José Alfredo Jiménez had made famous but I couldn't remember the words.

!!!

I dozed off and on for the next several hours. At one point Alicia announced that she had some errands to run and that if I got hungry again there was soup in the refrigerator. She said that the dogs would keep their eyes on me.

When I had tired of the cot I tried using my legs by walking around the room. In addition to the cot and computer, the room held a sewing machine, a couple of cardboard boxes stuffed with what I assumed were old clothes, a dinged-up bookshelf crammed with paperbacks—romances and science fiction—and the altar with the statue of Our Lady of Guadalupe.

At Our Lady's feet and strewn across the altar's table was a variety of odd objects: A ball point pen inscribed with the words "Colorado State Fair–1976"; a straight razor; a miniature bottle of Pancho Villa tequila; a 45 RPM recording of "Cherry Pink and Apple Blossom White" by Pérez Prado; and other mementos of life stories that had ended. The photographs on the altar had looked familiar to me when I had first seen them and the only reason for that was the ethnicity of the people in the pictures. They were all Mexicans. Old grandfathers and young nieces. Some of the photos were sepia-tinged with frames that were ornate and old-fashioned, others were basic Polaroids or school pictures. Prominently displayed in the center of the altar was a large photo of a motorcycle. A man with long hair in a ponytail and a young boy wearing a cowboy hat sat on the motorcycle. The boy's skinny arms reached around the man's waist. The picture-taker's shadow angled along the ground toward the motorcycle and I could deduce that a woman had snapped the photo.

I gingerly walked to the kitchen and stood in the doorway staring at the still-prancing dogs. The backyard was overgrown with weeds and the remnants of a vegetable garden dead from the summer heat. In a far corner a clump of colorful flowers had survived—geraniums, hollyhocks, even a rose or two. Near the chain link fence that marked the boundary between the yard and the alley sat a hulk as big as a small horse covered with a tarp anchored in the weedy ground. I pushed open the screen door and eased myself out among the dogs. My presence upset them but they weren't mad, just not sure how to act. They barked and yelped and jumped and got in my way as I shuffled to the tarp-covered hulk. I lifted a corner of the oily tarp and saw the motorcycle from the photograph.

I slowly made it back to the house and eventually crawled onto the cot where I waited for Alicia.

NINE

A DRY, HOT wind whipped the town of Pueblo for much of the time that Alicia pursued the mundane activities of her life away from the bar and her house. I complained to the dogs about the heat and they politely listened but for the most part they ignored the heat and the wind and looked at me like I was quite an oddball. But deep down we knew that we were brothers of circumstance—lost souls taken in by the woman who couldn't resist a sad-eyed mongrel with a busted paw, or a broken-up lawyer with a bad case of the blues.

Alicia returned around four, and the wind stopped but the heat remained. We warmed up the soup and each had a bowl. The warm broth of rice and chicken tasted good but did nothing to cool me off, although she had assured me that it would. I thanked her for taking care of me and she listened for a few minutes. She cut me off when I got long-winded with my gratitude.

She asked, "What else you got going besides getting beat up, drinking too much, and feeling sorry for yourself?"

"Gee, that about sums it up. That's me. How about you?"

"I know there's more to you than that, Móntez. But, if you don't want to reveal yourself, okay. Me? Not much, other than what you see." She spread her arms and took in the house, yard, and dogs with her reach. "My house, you see. My job, you know about. The crazy dogs, you've met. What else? Oh, yeah, I've been camped in Pueblo for about ten years. I've also been a waitress, a cashier at K-Mart, and I even did a little secretary work, for a lawyer, no less. I'm just a hardworking Chicana who takes in strangers, if they tell good stories, and they get their ass kicked in the front of Gordon's."

I laughed. "Don't make me laugh. Please. My ribs aren't up to it yet."

She gathered the soup bowls, placed them in the sink, and told me to grab a chair and follow her. She led me out the back door to a lawn chair resting under an old and leafy Elm tree. We were across the yard from the motorcycle. The evening air pressed in on us, sticky and heavy, so she went back in the house and returned with two glasses of lemonade.

As she handed me the drink she said, "I'd offer you a beer but you might not be able to handle it yet."

"Oh no," I said diplomatically. "This is good. Just what I need."

I tried some small talk. I said, "What happened to the garden? The heat?"

"Of course. Pueblo's always damn hot, but this year—it's been crazy. Too much water needed and with the restrictions–*ya 'stuvo*. Can't afford it. My flowers made it, though. Of course, they'll be gone soon. They're so fragile, but they lasted this long. They always surprise me, and then they leave."

We enjoyed the quiet time until the dogs started acting up. Alicia hollered at them, "Down, Baby! Shut up, Chato! Negra, get down!"

Her commands were useless. The dogs quit barking and jumping when they tired of the sport. Then they plopped themselves in the shade of the tree, too close for my own personal level of comfort but Alicia didn't appear to notice.

I said, "I didn't know I told any good stories. But, if you say so, okay. I guess I can also tell you that I like music, especially jazz, Chicano, R&B. I spend too much on CDs. There's a couple of ex-wives and a pair of boys out there somewhere, and I've been a lawyer for much too long. But maybe you knew that. I seemed to have already spilled my guts."

I laughed again but she didn't join me. She sat silently, clutching her glass of lemonade.

My words came out too loud.

"I saw the photograph on the altar. The man and the boy. That must have been rough. I made you think of something that you didn't want to."

She shook her head and reached across the space between our chairs to grab my hand.

She said, "Hey, Móntez. It's nothing you said. I think about them every day and this just happened to be the time. It's my own melodrama. Nick was my old man. And Ritchie was our boy. They were a team, those two. They loved that bike. Went for rides whenever they could."

She choked on her words.

I said, "That's okay. It's none of my business."

"It's all right, really. It's been years since they've been gone. I should be able to talk about it. And I can. Sure."

She let my hand drop.

"You probably think they died on that bike."

I nodded. The blood had drained from her face.

She continued. "That wasn't it. They were in a damn car. It had been raining and I didn't want Ritchie to get wet, and I didn't like it when Nick took him out for rides at night, especially when it's been raining, you know what I mean. They were coming back from a trip to the store, the grocery store. We needed milk and *tortillas*—"

She stalled at that point. I reached for her hand but she moved it to her lap.

When she spoke again, her voice had a higher pitch and the words came out strained and stripped of everything except their awful truth.

"And, and a guy ran a red light and hit them and—"

She stopped talking and stared at the motorcycle. She appeared to be holding her breath.

"God," I said. "What can I do?"

She shuddered. A thin smile crossed her pale lips.

"You can't do anything, but thanks for asking, Móntez. I'm all right, really. You're the one we should be worried about."

We finished our drinks and I doubt that we said another dozen words to each other. We had our own thoughts and hang-ups and problems and neither one of us was sure we could share any of them with the person sitting less than a foot away.

She finally stirred herself and trudged off to her job, leaving me to feed the dogs. I did what I could for the animals and then thought about calling Mariele Castilla but convinced myself that the call could wait.

I fretted that Rosa might try to find me in the valley and then worry when Michael Torres told her he hadn't seen me. She might call out the State Patrol to check every ravine and ditch between Denver and Antonito, and insist that they search La Veta Pass on foot. But I didn't want to talk with her because I would have to explain why I was holed up in Pueblo, and any explanation would only make her worry that much more. There was nothing I could say that would make her feel better about why I was still on the road.

Around seven, I called my office and left a message for Rosa on our answering machine on the assumption that she was compulsive enough to check the machine even when she was supposed to be off the clock. She had done it before. I let Rosa know where I was and that I was still on my way to the valley but that I hadn't made it yet. I gave her Alicia's address but not her phone number. I said nothing about my encounter with Tyler Boudin. She could think that I had picked up a woman and had changed my priorities. It would be easy for her to think that.

I looked in Alicia's refrigerator and found a can of cheap beer that I drank in about two minutes. I knew then that I could have driven to the valley that night. But I told myself that I should wait for her, that it was the decent thing to do.

I started a half-dozen of her paperbacks but they couldn't hold my attention and I didn't finish any. She didn't have a television and her radio was tuned to a country station that was too modern for my taste. When I tried to change the station, I found only static and buzz. I killed time spread out on the cot, staring at the ceiling or *La Virgen*.

The headlights of a car flashed through the house just as I was drifting toward sleep. At first I thought it was Alicia, but it was only midnight, which meant that she still had about three hours before she would be home. A car coming down the street, late at night, shouldn't have bothered me—but it did. I was sore and bruised and that had made me more careful. And paranoid. From the front door I watched a car park in front of the house. A man sat in the driver's seat of what looked like a black Lexus. There might have been another person in the passenger seat. I saw the glow of a cigarette lighter shine from inside the car but I couldn't make out any faces. I opened the door and walked to the car. What did I have to lose? I had already been beaten up. The car's engine started up. The headlights lit up the gravel of Alicia's lonely road and the Lexus pulled away. The only thing I saw with any clarity was the slogan on the rear license plate: **LAND OF ENCHANTMENT.**

⠿

She didn't argue all that much about my leaving. She said what she was supposed to say about me resting up, being careful, and "staying out of trouble." But just before noon she drove me to the bar so that I could continue with what she called my "strange journey."

I removed several parking tickets from the windshield and gave my car a few minutes to get over its lethargy from sitting for almost two days on black asphalt in Pueblo summertime heat. She leaned her head in the open window and said, "I'm still thinking about calling the cops. You were attacked outside my bar, my place of employment. It might be in my interests to get the cops in on this, let them patrol the street, keep an eye on things."

I nodded, reluctantly. "You should do what you think is right. Maybe you *should* have someone else work your shift with you for a few days. Better safe than sorry. But, to tell the truth, I doubt anything happens."

I wanted to sound sure of myself but there was a catch in my voice that even I heard. The black Lexus had me spooked although I had told her that it must have been a person looking for a street address. He had nothing to do with me or Tyler Boudin or the Santos family.

She kissed me on the cheek.

"Goodbye, Móntez, Denver lawyer. Stop by the bar on your way back. First one's on the house."

Then she turned her back and walked to her car.

I pulled away from Alicia and her dogs and her memories and headed south.

!!i

I went a little crazy on that drive. My mind was on a hundred different images, ideas, random thoughts. I had the music turned up way too loud but I didn't notice it until my ears ached. I stayed clear of traffic, speeding up and passing anything in the lanes ahead of me, and pulling over when somebody approached from behind, obviously in more of a hurry than I was. I can't recall the highway, the weather, the traffic. The trip was one long continuous blur and I was lucky that I wasn't stopped for speeding.

The mountains rose ahead of me as I left the flat, dry Pueblo basin. I drove through the old railroad and mining town of Walsenberg, stopped for gas, then whizzed past the shrine alongside Highway 160 without looking at the statue of the Virgin Mary or the crosses and crucifixes decorated with dying flowers. I climbed La Veta Pass and raced into the San Luis Valley. It was a drive I had made a hundred times before but I don't remember doing it that day I left Alicia in Pueblo to search out Fermín Santos and his need for revenge.

Mariele and Fermín had started me on this road and I could blame them for the beating I had received, as well as the feeling that I had landed in something that made no sense to me but that had the potential to screw me good. But I knew where the blame had to rest. I had to apologize to Harry López and Rolanda Alvarez, and even Mariele Castilla, and while I was at it I might as well try to convince Rosa that I did appreciate what she meant to my law business. When Alicia's name made it to the list, I quit. The names and the guilt added up faster than my driving.

Somewhere in all that the face of Freddie Canales appeared like a *papel picado* skeleton, floating in my car, laughing at the fools still living.

My car tires screamed. Heat waves wiggled across the horizon. Outside of Fort Garland, a snake sat in the middle of the highway, soaking up the heat. I swerved and missed it but in my rear view mirror I saw it crushed by an eighteen-wheeler. The air conditioner blasted my face and the plaintive crooning of Cornelio Reyna bounced inside the car.

My father often had expressed his opinion that I was a man who was disappointed if I didn't disappoint myself.

How can you argue with logic like that?

TEN

MARIELE CASTILLA FOUND me an hour after I checked into the Alamosa Inn. She breezed into the motel room with a hug and a kiss and a smile as bright as the valley sunshine. She didn't explain how she knew where I was and I didn't ask since it seemed like the most natural thing in the world that she would find me as soon as I made it to her town.

She sounded concerned when she asked, "What happened to you? Who did this?" She touched the bruised flesh around my eye.

I drew back from her hand.

"Easy. It's still sore. I got in a fight. The usual kind of thing. Too much beer and not enough sense."

Mariele sat down on the motel bed.

"Aren't you a little old for that game? You're such a guy, Louie."

"Now, *that's* funny. Somebody else told me that, not too long ago. I wonder what it means."

"It means that you should know better, that's all. How bad is it? Are you really hurt?"

I believed that she cared about my condition and that she was worried about the trouble I dragged around like a small boy hanging on to the last piece of his favorite blanket. But I didn't tell her about Tyler Boudin.

She looked good in her western woman outfit of jeans, a blouse with fringe, boots, and a floppy, wide-brimmed hat. She looked as good as the night in the Sagebrush, and I smiled because Mariele and I apparently had developed a habit of motel rooms.

She asked, "What's so funny? You like getting beat up? Is that it?"

She was a little too eager with her questions and I remembered that before Tyler Boudin had marked my body with his fists and boot heels, Mariele Castilla had done a pretty good job herself with her teeth and fingernails.

"No, nothing like that. I just had a thought, a reminder that you and I have a history but I really don't know anything about you. And I don't know what you expect me to do, now that I'm down here."

"What a strange thing to call it. A history. Is that what it was for you, Luis? Just another part of your history?"

I shrugged. Her face creased in a deep frown. She shook her head and forced a smile across her lips.

"Oh, that's all right. Call it whatever you want." She stretched on the bed and spoke to the ceiling. "Fermín finally gave me some information. The man he hired will be in town tomorrow. Dominic's funeral is set for tomorrow morning. He . . . his body arrives tonight from Denver. Fermín said that his man will finish business tomorrow night or the next day, depending on what he finds out about Barber's layout. If you talk with him tomorrow some time we still have a chance to stop this. I'll find out where this man is, leave that to me. Then the two of us can find him, try to buy him off, convince him to leave. If it works, great."

"And if it doesn't?"

She raised herself from the bed, leaned backwards, and rested on the support of her arms.

"Then I agree with what you said before. I'll go to the police, tell them everything and they can put Barber in protective custody or whatever they want to call it. This man, whoever he is, either he gets caught or he leaves when he sees that he doesn't have any opportunity."

"Mr. Santos will be arrested. You know that."

She paused. "Yes. I know. But what else can I do? That's why it's so important that we try whatever we can tomorrow, right after the funeral. That's why I need your help. I can't do this by myself. I *need* your help."

I didn't believe for a minute that there was anything that Mariele Castilla could not do by herself. But as long as she was willing to go to the cops if we couldn't stop Fermín's crazy plan, then I would do what I could to help her.

She extended her arms and invited me to the bed. I didn't move. Her smile vanished. She jumped from the bed and played with her hair.

She said, "No more 'sympathy,' is that it? Can't say that I'm surprised. I just expected more from you. Guess you're earning your retainer the old fashioned way?"

She must have meant that I was working for the old man's money and not her body. That bothered her.

I said, "It doesn't feel right. Dominic's not even buried yet. I'm not what you think, not what you need. And I don't think I need what you're offering either. Hate to be so blunt, but what else can I do? I'm afraid that I may have let things get out of hand and—"

I had been slapped by a woman before, more than once. There had been one night when I had been slapped by two different women. I eventually concluded that I deserved the slaps, that they were punishment for transgressions far worse than a temporary sting on my cheek. But when Mariele Castilla hit my face with the flat of her hand my head jerked in pain and surprise. Her lips peeled back over her teeth and her hair flew around her head like the raised fur of a cornered alley cat.

"Shut up! I don't want any explanation from you. I get the picture, Móntez. I understand. Better men than you have brushed me off."

She didn't give me any time to regroup. She rushed out of the room and slammed the door. I heard a pickup start up and then the squeal of her tires. Through the room's window I watched her leave and the scene reminded me of the night Fermín Santos had collapsed in my office and she had raced to the hospital.

I called my nephew.

When he answered I said, "Michael, this is Luis. I'm staying at the Alamosa Inn. I'll be around for a day or two. I'm working for Fermín Santos and Mariele Castilla. If something happens to me tell the cops to talk to Mariele."

He said, "What the hell are you talking about?"

I repeated, "If something happens to me the cops should talk to Mariele Castilla. She knows about my business down here and she can give them some ideas of who to look for."

"Damn, *tío*. This sounds crazy! What could happen to you? Are you all right?"

"Yeah, don't worry. This is all 'just in case.' I didn't want to worry you, but I thought I should let you know."

He wasn't convinced and neither was I. And what bothered me the most was that I wasn't sure if I told him about Mariele because she had information about Fermín's hit man or because of the way she had slapped me. I decided that afternoon that I didn't owe her an apology for anything.

░

I escaped the drab, cigarette-smelling motel room and walked along Highway 160, known as Main Street in Alamosa. The gift shops, restaurants, hardware stores, and *segundas* exploited the valley's natural beauty and the unnatural tourist trade. The street was busy with slow-moving traffic and the sidewalks had several window-shopping strollers but it was a small town afternoon, in the middle of the week, and I felt that the stores could close any minute, that someone could drop a curtain and the town could turn itself off and I would be left in darkness and loneliness.

In almost every store window, red and black, silk-screened posters announced a meeting about the water rights dispute:

SAVE THE VALLEY!
STOP THE THEFT OF OUR WATER AND
OUR HISTORY!

A group calling itself the San Luis Valley Water Rights Council asked all those "concerned about the future of the survival of the San Luis Valley way of life" to attend the meeting set for the next Saturday at 7:00 p.m. in the S.P.M.D.T.U.

Hall in Antonito. Among the lengthy list of scheduled speakers were the names Fermín Santos and Mariele Castilla.

I continued to walk and eventually I found myself in front of the old courthouse. It didn't look busy, not even open. But it triggered a memory of Freddie Canales, a man who had turned up in my car on the drive to the valley and now a man who interrupted my aimless wandering in a small Colorado town.

Canales had been my one, true heartbreak client. A young man whose only crime might have been overreacting to another man's bullying, Canales had been sentenced to very hard time by a judge who thought all young Chicanos had the potential, as well as a penchant, to turn into gangsters, killers, and thieves, and it was his duty to keep them locked up for as long as the system would allow. I had represented Canales as a favor to the public defender's office, who at the time of the Canales trial was defending Canales's alleged victim in another case. During the trial I presented evidence that I thought clearly showed that Canales had a reasonable belief that he was under siege by Joseph "Joey" Rodríguez.

Rodríguez and Canales lived in the same low-income housing complex and their families had feuded since before Freddie had been born. The two men had fought each other for years and Freddie Canales had usually received the worst of it. Freddie was a smiling, joking eighteen-year-old kid who thought that he could one day do something with his natural skill at cartoon-drawing. Rodríguez was a loud, muscle-bound jerk who tormented anyone he wanted. One cold night, in the housing complex's parking lot, Canales decided that he'd had enough of Rodríguez's torment, but he had to use a tire iron to make his point. Rodríguez was in a coma for a week. That was too much for the district attorney, who refused to offer any deal that made sense; for the jurors, who were convinced by the DA's rhetorical implications that their own lives would be safer if they found Canales guilty; and for the judge, who concluded that the "aggravating circumstances" of Freddie's life required him to impose all the sentence he could. I guess those circumstances were that Freddie was a poor boy without much going for himself except a good sense of humor and a family who loved him.

Freddie Canales lost his smile when the judge sentenced him to fifteen years. Rodríguez woke from the coma healthier and meaner than ever, ended up in prison the same time as Freddie, and the feud continued. I visited Freddie on a regular basis for the first few years of his incarceration and I watched as he gradually became a sullen, withdrawn, angry con. He finally refused to see me. The Canales family celebrated with a huge party when he was paroled, and I attended that party but it was obvious to his family that although he had been freed from prison, Freddie Canales was still locked-up, still behind bars.

A week after he was released, Freddie challenged the Denver cops, and Freddie lost that fight, too.

I told myself that I should eat something and I walked into the Purple Pig with that idea but all I had in the bar was a tall glass of bourbon and Coke and a trio of beer chasers. My real intention for going to the bar, as it turned out, was to mull over my life since I had encountered Mariele Castilla, Fermín Santos, and the San Luis Valley water war. I accepted that I had let guilt drive too many of my recent decisions but that acceptance didn't clear up anything for me.

I quit the thinking and decided that I had to try some action. I had to talk with Fermín Santos.

!!i

The Santos ranch covered several acres about thirty miles from Alamosa on the edge of the Great Sand Dunes National Monument. *Chamiso hediondo*—blue sage— piñon trees, and cactus dotted the earth, and a clear stream of cold water cut through the middle of the ranch. A sign said that I was on the Santos Ranch Road. I saw rabbits, a lone coyote, several hawks and a lost-looking pair of antelope. I encountered only one other car, and that was in my rear view mirror. It came from the opposite direction, on another road that forked into the Santos Ranch Road and then headed in the direction of town. In the darkness and the limited view of my mirror it looked like a black Lexus but I couldn't be sure.

I drove under a wooden archway decorated with white deer and elk antlers. A faded sign on the archway proclaimed:

TIERRA DE LOS SANTOS–HOLY EARTH. The house was a few miles further up the road and when I saw lights, I drove the car off the road and parked. I wanted to approach the house without being seen and learn what I could of the lay of the land, and if anyone else was visiting the old man that night.

I walked through scrub bushes and stumbled over mounds that I finally figured out were anthills. The warm valley night was quiet and peaceful and when the moon broke through the clouds I had no trouble seeing my way to the wood chip path that led to the front door of the house. I saw only a pickup and recognized it as the one that the old man and Mariele had arrived in at my office. When I was within twenty yards of the front door, a large dog raced from the rear of the house. It barked and snarled at me, and snapped at my legs. I tried to calm it down by talking to it but my words only made it angrier. It didn't attack but it prevented me from moving forward. The dog held its ground and I couldn't go in any direction except backwards.

The door opened and Fermín Santos said, "Who's there? *¿A quién busca?* What do you want?"

His silhouette filled the pale yellow rectangle of the doorway and I could see that he held a rifle in his hands.

"It's Luis Móntez, Mr. Santos. The lawyer from Denver. I want to talk with you."

"What? What are you doing here? Where's your car? I didn't see any lights."

"Your dog, Mr. Santos. Can you call him off?"

The old man hollered, "*¡Paquito! ¡Silencio!*"

The dog whimpered, sniffed my legs one more time then ran back to the old man, who had made his way off the porch and onto the wood chips.

"Come in, Mr. Móntez."

The dog returned to where it had come from and I followed Santos into the house. I watched him carefully place the rifle against a wall near the doorway.

Except for the glow of a light from a rear room, the house was in darkness. The old man flipped a switch to turn on a hanging lamp.

He quietly said, "Have a seat. Please."

I sat on a leather couch and the furniture groaned under my weight as though no one had used it for years. Nearby, small piles of sympathy cards lay on the floor near a rocking chair. There must have been more than a hundred cards strewn across the highly polished hardwood parquet.

He remained standing. With each move of my body the leather squeaked. I hoped that he would offer me a drink.

I said, "I'm sorry about your son. And your health. How are you doing?"

Santos made his way to the rocking chair. He pushed a clump of cards out of his way with the toe of his boot and sat down. The rocking chair also squeaked. He looked older than the strong, confident man who had raged about Matthew Barber until he had collapsed in my office. His face had lost some of its tan but had gained a gray covering of stubble and his hair was out of place, disheveled, and ignored.

The chair moved with a slow, gentle rock. He took a half-smoked cigarette from his shirt pocket and stuck it in his mouth, rolled his tongue around the tip, and then held it in his fingers.

He said, "Thank you for your concern, Mr. Móntez." He paused and it looked to me as though he puffed on the unlit cigarette stub. "I'm an old man, a *viejo*. I've fought all my life for my family, my land, and I've fought against old age. But, now I know I don't have much time left, and I don't really care about the aches or pains that this body gives me. The pain of losing my son—that is something that has finally made me stop. Everything. The fight is over. I've lost. I wait for *la muerte*."

"I, uh, I . . ." There was nothing I could say.

He tossed the stub and shook his head. "No, *señor*, don't worry yourself about me, and don't think you have to comfort me. I am, at last, at peace. Strange, no? *Pero, si es la verdad*."

He leaned back in the rocker. "Now, what can I do for you? You didn't come all the way out here to tell me that you are sorry about Dominic's death. You could have sent a card, like these." His boot knocked over one of the small piles of cards. "And you must have parked down the road so that you could walk up without being seen. You're either up to no good or you are afraid of something. What is it, Mr. Móntez?"

"Actually, I'm here because Mariele and I are worried that you may be involved in something that can only lead to disaster. Although she doesn't know I'm here. I'm being careful because I've already been threatened. I think that what you are trying to do is very dangerous, and foolish. I'm here to try to convince you to call off the man you hired."

"I have no idea what you are talking about. I've hired no man, as you put it. Hired to do what? Dangerous? Foolish? What are you talking about, Móntez?"

He stared at me and I stared at him. I tried to read his face, his eyes, the way he gripped the arms of the rocker.

"I'm talking about the man you hired to avenge Dominic's killing. The man you hired to kill Matthew Barber. You have to call him off. You have to stop whatever it is that you've started."

The chair stopped rocking. He slowly raised himself from the chair and stood as close to me as he could. His boots bumped against my shins. He was shaking.

"Get out, Móntez. You will have to leave. You've insulted me, and my grief over Dominic. I told you, the fight is over. I have no idea where you got your wild fantasy about me hiring anyone, or why you thought you could come here and tell me all this nonsense, but now you have to leave."

He moved away from me, back to the wall. He picked up the rifle and cradled it in his arms.

"Get out, Móntez. Now."

"Mr. Santos, please. Maybe there's something I can do, something we both can do. Let me—"

He aimed the rifle at my heart. He said, "Leave, Móntez, now. Without another word."

I jumped off the couch and walked backwards to the front door, keeping my eye on him. I stretched my hands to him, half raised in surrender, half in a futile gesture meant to deflect anything he might shoot at me with his weapon. I left his house just like he ordered, without another word.

ELEVEN

I HAD DRIVEN about three miles on the Santos Ranch Road when a pair of headlights swung into view behind me. I accelerated my car but they stayed in my rearview mirror, faded by dust but still constant and persistent. I gradually increased my speed on the loose gravel. A couple of times my car fish-tailed and jerked, almost out of control, but I drove not thinking about what might happen if I did lose it, if I was forced to stop because I had run off the road into a ditch or a patch of brush.

I tried to see who was driving but I could make out only the unclear figure of a man wearing a cap. The car was a dark Lexus.

He didn't try to pass or run me off the road. He kept a steady pace, speeding up when I did, slowing down when I had to because of the terrain. He was letting me know that he was watching me, that there wasn't a place I could go without him knowing about it, and that if he wanted he could stop me. I tore through the countryside, twisting with the curves of the road, bouncing over the rocks and ruts, and all the time acutely aware of the headlights.

I approached the intersection of the Santos Ranch Road and Highway 160, where I would be back on asphalt, able to turn up my speed but also more vulnerable. He could pass and wait for me up ahead or stay on my ass and force me to make a mistake on the highway.

I pressed even harder on the gas pedal as the highway

appeared ahead. Another pair of headlights approached from the west on the highway. As I drew closer to the intersection I saw that the approaching vehicle was a semi-truck, an eighteen-wheeler with a long trailer. A yellow and black sign warned me about highway traffic, and a stop sign commanded me to let the highway traffic through.

I didn't stop, didn't slow down. I raced through the intersection and streaked in front of the truck, whose horn cried out in the night and whose brakes screamed as the trucker swerved to avoid me. I burst ahead with more speed but the trucker had slowed down. Somewhere behind the semi, the Lexus also had to slow down and for a few seconds the truck separated my car from the man who had been following me. Headlights glared at me from the opposite direction—the Lexus would have to sit behind the trucker for another minute or two. Another road opened to my right. I flipped off my car lights and banked into the side road. I drove onto the shoulder and stopped the car. The truck sped by with a roar and behind it the Lexus followed, waiting for its chance to pass. I sat there for twenty minutes, expecting somebody, anybody.

Tyler Boudin had warned me off of his business with a beating whose effects still caused me to groan when I twisted the upper half of my body. Fermín Santos had denied knowing anything about any hit man, and he had warned me off *his* business with a rifle that I did not doubt he knew how to use quite well. But the person who made me sweat while I sat in the darkness of my car on a deserted dirt road was someone who had been watching me since the night at Alicia's, someone about whom I knew absolutely nothing except that he traveled in an expensive car and he knew at all times where I was and what I was doing.

I unbuckled my seat belt, switched off the overhead light so that it wouldn't go on when I opened the door, and eased out of the driver's door. I searched the immediate area and made sure that I was off the road and out of the way. Then I climbed in the backseat and lay down. I had decided not to return to the motel, and not to take any chances on the lonely streets and roads of the San Luis Valley, at least not that night. I curled up the best I could and waited for the morning, mostly not sleeping, trying not to think about the mess I had made of the situation, trying not to dwell on the bad choices I had made, trying not to imagine that every car I heard on the road or the highway was a dark colored Lexus carrying a passenger who knew more about me than I would ever know about him. And I tried not to think about Mariele Castilla and her lies, deceptions and schemes.

⠇⠇

I drove into town in fresh morning air and warm sunshine and I felt better about things, except for the soreness and general aches from my encounter with Boudin and my night cramped in the backseat of my car. I stopped at my motel, stuck a chair under the door knob, ran through a shower and changed my clothes. I checked out, ordered an instant breakfast at a drive-through hamburger stand, and decided between visiting my nephew, Michael Torres, or paying my respects to Dominic Santos at his funeral mass. I finished tasteless ham and cheese in a tasteless croissant then drove to a convenience store where I parked in front of a row of telephones. I stood by a phone watching the street, waiting.

My first call was to Michael.

"Why don't you come by the house? What have you been up to? How come all these phone calls? Are you okay?"

"Easy, Michael. I don't think I can stop by, this visit. I've got to get back to Denver. But, have there been any messages for me? Anyone call?"

"Oh, yeah. You're a popular guy. Your secretary, Rosa? Worried as hell that you hadn't made it to my house. I told her you were doing all right, but I don't know if you are."

"Yeah, yeah, I'm okay. If she calls back tell her I'll be back in town by the weekend. She can call me at my house. Who else?"

He said, "Hang on a minute." I heard him put the phone down and a minute later pick it back up. "Here it is. A woman named Alicia Aragón. I guess you gave her my name. Said she was a friend and hoped that you had found time to rest. She sounded worried when I told her that you hadn't stopped by. She also said to tell you that she took your advice and is laying low. In fact, she's going to take some time off. Not sure why she told me that. Man, you are out there, *tío*. All these women checking up on you like a little lost puppy that everyone's looking for." He asked again, "Are you sure you're okay?"

The answer, of course, was no, I most definitely was not okay. I had been sleeping in my car, afraid to go to my nephew's house and get him caught up in something that I didn't understand, and afraid to return to my motel room because who knew who might be waiting for me there. And I had become involved with a woman who had lied to me about a wild plot that her father-in-law had supposedly concocted, and her lies had staked me out in the cross hairs of a rogue undercover federal drug agent.

I said, "Yes, Michael. I'm really all right. Do not worry, please. If either Rosa or Alicia calls again, tell them that I'm on my way back. I'll stop by and visit Alicia. For sure, she does not have to worry about me."

"Whatever, Louie. Just be careful, man. You get in some crazy stuff. If you need help, you know how to reach me."

I walked inside the store and bought myself a cup of coffee. When I was outside again I found a folded piece of paper in my wallet that had Alicia's home phone number. My second call was to her.

I hung up after ten rings. No answer, no answering machine, no voice messaging. It was too early for her to be at the bar. She must have been at the grocery store, buying dog food for her pets. Or, she had started her "time off" that we had supposedly talked about, although I could not remember that conversation, and she had left town. That's what I told myself as I climbed back in my car and tried to figure out what my next step was in what my bartender friend had called my "strange journey."

I felt the gun against my neck before it actually touched my skin. I tried to turn around but the guy holding the gun wrapped a hand around my mouth.

"Don't say or do anything or I will shoot you. You're going to drive and I'm going to tell you where to go. Understand?"

He released his hold on my mouth. I said, "I understand. What do you want?"

"Go down Main until you see the sign for Antonito. Get on

that road and drive until I tell you to turn off. Keep your eyes on the road and shut up."

The guy was too polite to be Tyler Boudin. What I could see of his face in my rear view mirror confirmed my assumption that someone other than Boudin had taken an interest in my trip to the San Luis Valley. He was *indio*-looking with squinty eyes, round forehead and a sharp nose, in his thirties most likely, wearing very dark sunglasses and a blue baseball cap with an embroidered grinning wolf and white lettering that said **"Los Lobos–Peace, Ese"**—a man with an ironic sense of humor.

I followed his directions and in about twenty minutes we were in a stand of pine and scrub, surrounded by boulders that blocked us from the view of anyone not in the stand itself.

He ordered me out of the car and we walked to a shady spot, up against one of the giant rocks near a gnarled, wind-bent piñon tree.

He sat on an outcropping of chiseled limestone that protruded from the massive boulder and motioned for me to sit on the ground where he could keep an eye on me.

He said, "You can call me Emilio. I don't have anything against you, although you might not believe that right now. The gun and theatrics maybe weren't needed but I can't be too careful. Someone sent me a message. The message was that you wanted to talk with me, that it had something to do with Dominic Santos and Fermín Santos. I'm very curious about what it is that you would want to say to me, especially as you don't know me, don't know anything about me."

"I can't talk with a gun aimed at me. Can you put it down?"

He pointed the bulky, ugly weapon towards the ground but he kept his finger on the trigger. That was all he was willing to give me.

I said, "You've been following me. Why?"

His grin stretched from Antonito to San Acacio.

"I'm a curious person. A lawyer I don't know wants to talk with me, I need to find out a few things about him, don't you think? By the way, how was it sleeping in the backseat of that car? I almost stopped and talked to you when I saw you parked on that side road, but I didn't want to spook you any more than you already were. You let a good motel room go to waste, brother." First impressions can be important, and my first impression of Emilio was that he was a wise ass and a bit twisted.

I said, "I assume you are the person that Mariele thinks old man Santos hired."

"Who hired me is not important," he answered, a bit uneasy.

I shrugged and said, "I don't care, really. You could be working for Mariele, the cops, anybody except Santos. The more I think about it, the less I believe Fermín Santos knows anything about you. I had thought that talking with you would save the old man some trouble, some very serious trouble. Now, it doesn't seem to matter. For whatever reason, someone, Mariele, wanted me to find you. Or for you to find me, I guess. As you can see, that has taken place. What happens next is anybody's bet."

He held the .357 Magnum loosely, almost carelessly, almost forgotten. It was a Desert Eagle with wood grips and a matte chrome finish. He scratched his thigh with its six-inch barrel. The sound of metal rubbing against the denim of his jeans filled the hollow and shut out the humming insects, the chirping birds, and the occasional automobile scattering dust on the road a few miles from where we sat.

Sweat trickled along my bruised ribs and on my forehead. I wanted to reach in my back pocket for my handkerchief, to wipe my face. I kept my hands in front of my body, where he could see them.

He said, "I think I understand. I wish I could help you, Móntez. But I'm an employee basically, at the service of my client. You being a lawyer, you must understand about client loyalty? I can't tell you what you need to know, and I'm worried that I've been compromised, put in a place that I shouldn't be. Can't blame you for that, though, and you don't have anything to do with my job. At least, not yet. As long as you stay out of my business."

"I'm done with any business you may have, Emilio. All I want is to get out of here and back to Denver, back to a place I know and understand, and people who don't talk in riddles, and where lies have more to do with love than hate."

He smiled, then he laughed.

"Móntez, you're almost a poet. A damn philosopher."

He stretched himself off the ledge and started walking in the direction of a black Lexus that had been parked on a hill overlooking us as we talked. He jammed his gun behind the belt that held up his pants, like the young punk in a B movie, and again I thought he was one careless bad guy.

"You go back to your big city, Móntez. The country can be a dangerous place for those who don't understand it, respect it. Forget about Santos and Mariele. And forget that you ever met me, okay?"

He didn't wait for an answer. He reached the top of the hill in less time than it took me to start up my car, turn it around, and head for the road. He opened the passenger side door and climbed into the Lexus, and then he was gone. He and his car and his driver disappeared behind the hill.

TWELVE

THE CADILLAC LOOMED like Moby Dick magically beached and dying on the sandy soil of a sea that had receded and dried up thousands of years ago. It appeared to dwarf Michael's small house. I thought of every terrible conclusion that I could jump to about the undeniable fact that Alicia's car was parked in front of my nephew's home.

Alicia and Michael sat on the peeling, white porch on white plastic chairs that I was sure Michael had picked up at the weekly flea market. They were drinking cans of Bud Light, and one of Michael's young daughters sat on the floor near them, playing with several toys that Burger King had used as a gimmick to entice children to demand a Kid's Meal.

I casually waved at them as I stepped up to the porch, grabbed an unopened beer from a cooler that had no ice, and had myself a long, tepid drink before I said a word.

When I came up for air, I said, "Hi, Alicia. What's new?"

She tried to laugh. Michael grunted.

She said, "I took that vacation and here I am. Called Michael to see if you ever made it. He said you phoned a while back, that you were talking crazy, something about that Castilla woman. I came by to see if you showed up, in case you need some help. Michael and I have been visiting, enjoying some beers, and listening to little Donna tell us all about her favorite movie, El Dorado."

On cue, Donna held up the plastic figures she had been pushing along the wooden floor. They included a blonde soldier wearing conquistador armor, a bosomy Indian maiden wearing almost nothing, and a fat Indian chief holding a golden goblet.

I laughed when Michael told his daughter to run off the porch and play in the lawn. There couldn't have been more than three square inches of grass anywhere near Michael's house, but for him the dirt and gravel equaled a lawn. If he had wanted to, and if he had taken care of it, and if there had been enough water, a lush green layer of grass could have carpeted his yard, and the possibility was enough for him. One day he would have a lawn in his front yard. For now he had the land and dozens of bushes of *chamiso hediondo*. Michael's life was based on possibilities.

I took another drink of beer.

"You may be right. I might need some help. Things have drifted a little out of hand."

"Careened, more like it. If you're in trouble, you need to tell us. I filled Michael in about that guy who beat you up. And what you said about him probably being a cop, a narc. And he's told me more about the Santos Ranch and Matthew Barber and the fight that's been going on down here for years. What are you going to do?"

Michael interrupted, "You got to go to the police. That guy working you over, and this crap with Mariele and Barber and the old man. You're in over your head, *tío*. Way over."

"If I go to the police, the only one who gets in trouble is the old man. He doesn't know a thing. And I don't know anything about the guy Mariele hired except the car he rides around in. But, that may be enough, actually. Can't be too hard to find a black Lexus around here."

Alicia strained forward, trying to understand my rambling. "What guy? Who you talking about, Móntez?"

Another drink. I had finished the twelve ounces.

"The guy I thought was a hit man hired by old man Santos. Not so, I learn. More likely Mariele hired him, since she seemed to know a lot about him. For some reason, she wanted me to talk with him, make sure he knew I knew about him. Well, he knows.

But what he's up to, I don't have a clue. And why Mariele wanted us to get together is an even bigger puzzle."

Now Michael leaned forward in his seat. He said, "The hit man, or whatever, he talked with you?"

"Yeah. Just a little while ago. He said he had heard that I wanted to talk with him, but he didn't say who he heard that from. Must have been Mariele. She also said that old man Santos had hired someone to revenge his son's death, but when I talked with Fermín, he almost shot me because I insulted him by simply uttering anything like that."

It was Alicia's turn. "You talked with the old man?"

"Yeah, but it didn't get me anything, except chased off the road, and a bad night's sleep in the back of my car."

Michael stood up and grabbed my elbow. He ushered me to his chair and made me sit down.

"Start from the beginning, Louie. What the hell have you been up to?"

The process required another six-pack and another hour, but eventually Alicia sat back in her chair and Michael plopped on the splinters of his porch floor, and they each said that they finally understood. Trouble was, I sure as hell didn't.

!!!

Michael offered his opinion that the so-called hit man sounded too slipshod, too easy-going to be a killer for hire. A professional wouldn't treat the tool of his trade in the cavalier fashion that I had described, and, Michael noted, the guy had been too much out front, too much in the open to be what I thought he was and what he had tried to pass himself off as.

"What hired gun rides around in a black Lexus, a car everyone's going to notice, especially down here in the valley? And the clumsy way he let you see him in Pueblo, and out by old man Santos's place? It doesn't add up, Louie. Doesn't compute, as my kids used to say."

"Tell me something I don't know, nephew."

"We should get together with Bobby Treviño, my pal on the police force. Bobby will listen to your story, ask Mariele a few questions, most likely warn Barber."

Alicia added, "And try to find the guy driving around in the Lexus. But what about Mr. Santos?" Michael was into his idea and he had an answer for everything.

"Bobby's smart. He won't do anything except what he has to. He's got to make a living around here, you know. He'll understand that the old man is upset. And from what you say, Santos is pretty convincing that he didn't have anything to do with bringing this guy to the valley."

Alicia nodded in agreement.

I said, "Mariele takes the fall?"

He shrugged with his shoulders and his lips.

While Michael made the call Alicia and I helped ourselves to another beer.

The day had turned god awful hot. In the blazing light of the unfiltered sun, my eyes played tricks on me. Sixty miles to the west a dust storm rolled along the foot of the San Juan Mountains like a bouncing clump of dirty cotton. The pale, white sky shimmered over our heads. Red-tailed hawks floated against the gleaming backdrop as though they had flown in that atmosphere for a thousand years, as though they would never touch earth again. I pressed the beer can against my cheek and I felt the aluminum accept the warmth of my face. My body ached, my muscles were ragged and sore, and I knew that whatever I had been thinking had not been complete but there was nothing I could do about it.

Alicia smiled and I tried to smile back. Her face was as dry and tight as the smothering air that engulfed Michael's house. Her hair hung loose around her shoulders, and the man's shirt and torn jeans she wore also hung loosely on her frame but in my weary, strained eyes she looked bundled and packaged, too hot for the weather.

She said, "I'm surprised I'm here, and thanks for asking, by the way."

I started to sputter something but she waved me into silence.

"It's all right, Móntez. I thought I had given up on guys like you, thought I had learned my lesson. And, yet, here I am. I can't explain it but it's not important for me to have an explanation. I guess it's only important that I'm here."

The screen door slammed against the rickety frame. Michael stood before us, his mouth open, waiting for the precise second when he should speak. His hands shook at his sides.

Alicia went to him.

"What is it? What's wrong?"

"They've been killed. Bobby just told me. This morning. They didn't show up for Dominic's funeral, didn't even check on the body last night when it finally arrived from Denver. So someone went out to the ranch to check on them. They found them. They're dead."

The glare of the summer day dimmed to a charcoal gray. I closed my eyes and listened to Alicia ask Michael the question.

"Who's dead, Michael?"

"The old man. And Mariele Castilla. Both of them. Shot at the old man's ranch."

"Oh, God! When?"

"They think last night, or early this morning. I can't believe it. Both of them. Killed like that."

Alicia's voice cracked.

"Killed like what, Michael? What do you mean?"

"They were together. In the house. But together. That's the way they found them. In bed. Naked. Together."

Alicia groaned.

I opened my eyes and saw Michael's ashen face, framed by the limpid sky. Out of view I heard the laughter of the little girl. Alicia stared at the vast, broad San Luis Valley. We waited for the policeman to come to talk to us.

THIRTEEN

THE THREE OF us needed the rest of the day to explain what we did and didn't know to Bobby Treviño and his pals. They were frazzled because multiple murders just did not happen in the San Luis Valley. The place had its share of crime and violence—what place didn't? But the murders of Fermín Santos and Mariele Castilla were different—colder, methodical, apparently not crimes of passion, which are a lot easier to figure out and solve than execution-style killings. The cops were visibly upset and they dealt with us in what they must have thought was a business-like, professional manner, but we could smell the fear of small town cops who might be out of their league.

The fact that the two victims were in bed together would titillate reporters all the way to Los Angeles and New York so Treviño had to be careful about that, too. Reputations are held dearly in the San Luis Valley and any cop worth his badge was not going to stumble over the remains of someone's good name if he could help it.

When Treviño tired of hearing our stories repeated, he warned us that we had to let him know if we planned to leave the valley. That was easy. Both Alicia and I were heading home as soon as we could and we gave him all the digits and words he needed including addresses, phone numbers and Alicia's email listing.

When I started to tell him goodbye, Michael grabbed my hand and held it. His brown eyes worked their way into mine.

"*Tío. Por favor.* You keep me informed. Anything I can do, any help you need, you call on me. My mother didn't teach me much but she always did say that you were the one person she could count on, even when she didn't deserve it. Now, I'm here for you. Don't lock me out. Keep me in the loop."

Then he gave me a quick *abrazo*, another one to Alicia, and we were on our way.

I followed her for two hours to Pueblo, never letting her out of my sight, staring at the Cadillac's massive rear window to prevent it from floating away before my eyes and hanging on her bumper until she pulled over in a rest stop and angrily told me to stay back. We arrived at her house tense and weary, sure that we would not be able to sleep.

We sat in her kitchen drinking sodas from her refrigerator. She said she didn't have anything else to offer and I went along with the lie. On Michael's porch she had let me know that she thought I was on the verge of losing the contest to drinking, whatever that contest was. I hadn't realized I had even submitted an entry.

"I'll pick up my dogs from the kennel in the morning," she explained. "Poor things, they must be going nuts. This is the first time I've done that."

"I can't tell you how bad I feel about getting you into this."

She vigorously shook her head.

"Don't, Móntez. Don't apologize any more. I'm not doing anything I don't want to. The guy that beat you up in Gordon's parking lot dragged me into this, if you want to put it that way. I went to Alamosa on my own, my choice. I wanted to help you. I was worried about you. I care about you. You dropped in my life like a wounded stray and I can't let you go now. So, this is my thing. I just hope I don't make it worse, whatever the hell it is."

She looked out to her yard, wistful about the absent pets, I thought.

"Your nephew, Michael. He seems to have it together. Living the life he wants, where he wants. Seemed happy."

"Michael's always struck me that way, too. Although, he's

had hard times and money has been a consistent problem for him and his family. Can't get that one decent, long-term job so that he can get ahead. When he does work for a while, one of his kids gets sick, or the house needs a new furnace, or his truck throws a rod. He's not working now, you know."

"Really? He seemed to be doing all right. Waiting for you, we talked, and he gave me the impression that he was in good shape, financially. He said he was going to look into the chance to buy some more land. Need money for that."

"You hear that kind of talk in the valley. Folks dream about more land, more space, even though they already live in the wild, open country. For some of them, Alamosa is too much of a city, too closed in. And for Michael, dreaming about something is like having a plan about how to get it. But hell, what do I know?"

She finished her orange soda, opened the refrigerator and took out a can of cola and a plastic bottle of fruit juice. Through the open door and over her shoulder I saw a six pack of Miller Lite meekly waiting on the top refrigerator shelf.

"What can we know, Móntez? The older I get, the less I feel I know. I know that my dogs need to be fed and watered and walked, and that they won't listen to me unless they want to. I know that the flowers in my back yard will bloom every year, if I give them any attention at all, but then they die. Dry up and die. They're gone by now, I'd bet. Too much heat, not enough water, not enough of what they need in the soil. They're beautiful, fragile, transient. Just like so many other things in life."

She paused. I didn't want to interrupt whatever it was that she felt she needed to say.

"Yesterday, Mariele Castilla was alive and breathing the clean air of the San Luis Valley. She was tough, strong, but she turned out to be as temporary as my flowers."

A single tear ran down her cheek. We were both exhausted. Our nerves were frayed. I reached across the table and covered her hands with mine.

She looked at my hands over hers. "I've loved only one man my entire life. Nick, my 'biker daddy'." She tried to laugh but it didn't happen. "I thought he was going to be with me forever.

I thought Nick and Ritchie were going to be my life. I wonder if Mariele Castilla ever felt that way about anybody. If she had the chance to know love? Every person should have that chance, don't you think, Móntez?"

"Some can't know it. Some don't let themselves know it. But, Alicia, it can happen more than once."

She smiled. Her eyes shimmered with tears and the soft light over her sink.

"I don't think I can ever fall in love again. It's not going to happen. The only myths I believe in have to do with *La Llorona* and *La Virgen de Guadalupe* and *Aztlán*. Not love. Not the goddamn myth of love."

She shuddered.

"God, how pathetic! I'm starting to sound as forlorn as a drunk Denver lawyer I helped out one night. Now, he was in bad shape."

"Yeah, that's pretty bad. Watch out for those lawyers."

She shuddered again, stood up.

She said, "I'm going to need help getting to sleep tonight."

Alicia walked away. I waited at the kitchen table. I heard her shuffle into the bathroom. A minute passed, then the toilet flushed. A few more minutes passed. The door to the bathroom opened then shut. I followed her through the house and to the back bedroom.

I found her sitting on the edge of her bed. I sat next to her and kissed her. Her lips were shy and cold and the kiss was more of a gesture than an emotion. I hugged her, forgot about kissing or anything else and sat there on the bed with her in my arms. She cried quietly for Nick and Ritchie, the people who were supposed to be her life, and for people she never met, Fermín and Mariele. We stayed like that for several minutes. She didn't say anything and eventually the quiet crying stopped.

She kissed me again. The kiss was nothing like the first one. It was sweet and intense, direct and unforgiving. She swept me up in the fever of her love-starved heart, and when we removed each other's clothes and swarmed over each other's bodies it was as if we had been loving since *La Llorona* had cried for the first time for her dead children, since *La Virgen* had whispered prayers in the ears of Juan Diego, since *Aztlán* had been abandoned by our ancestors.

"How fortunate that neither one of us believes in love. This could get complicated, otherwise."

"I never said I didn't. That was you, lady. You called it a myth, as I recall."

"So, is this love?"

"You think it's a good idea to ask me things like that, after what we just did? I could say something really crazy, really emotional . . ."

"Really honest? Wouldn't want that, would we?"

I moved across her hips and started kissing her lips, her face, her neck. What was honest? What did I know about that? I didn't even know what was real. Except for Alicia on the bed with me. Alicia in my arms, Alicia making love to me, and me making love to her. That was real. As real as it could be.

Myths could be real, couldn't they? Or maybe it was truth. Myths could be true. That would do for me. Alicia was true. Together we found truth that night.

Part Three
The Hit Man and The *Pendejo*

FOURTEEN

FOR SEVERAL WEEKS the deaths of the old man and his son's girlfriend caught national attention. *Sixty Minutes* did a segment on the San Luis Valley water war with the clever title of "The Real Milagro Beanfield War." Ed Bradley tried to develop the theory, unconvincingly, I thought, but believed by almost everyone in the valley, that Matthew Barber had arranged for the killing of the old man because of Fermín's fierce resistance to Barber's business schemes and that Mariele had been an unfortunate witness.

The San Luis Valley Water Rights Council staged weekend marches through the streets of Alamosa and up the Sangre de Cristo Water Company road to Barber's locked gate. Max Macías's face showed up on the late news as a spokesman for the Council and the remaining members of Fermín's family. Each time I saw him on television speaking to a gathering of the press or on the steps of the Alamosa courthouse he looked thinner and weaker but his voice remained strong and eloquent. If Max was going out, he was leaving with grace and a fire he hadn't exhibited in several years. Max managed to get the ear of the state's Attorney General, a local valley boy who had made good in the big city, and, a month after the killings, a state grand jury was impaneled to investigate the murders, the water rights issues, and Barber's alleged role in both. No one expected any results from that investigation for at least six months.

Three months later the murders of Mariele Castilla and Fermín Santos were no more than an occasional topic on a radio talk show. Justice for Fermín and Mariele languished, and life for the rest of us went on, such as it was.

The Alamosa cops and eventually the Colorado Bureau of Investigation had a hard time with my story about the hit man, especially since I couldn't name the person he was supposed to be working for or offer any rational explanation for his actions. No one else had reported a black Lexus prowling the country roads of the valley, and no one seriously believed that Fermín Santos, one of the most respected elders in the valley, could have had anything to do with such a man. Mariele was another story, of course, and from the questions I was asked by the various law enforcement types, I pieced together that she, too, had a record, and that she also had been a suspect in the fire at the Barber cabin. Dominic's county jail death had closed the file on the arson case and the murder of Kyle Alarid, just as Mariele's death had closed all ears to any story I tried to tell about what I thought were the intricacies of the infamous water war. Ed Bradley didn't try to interview me, which was fine with me, and the attention I had drawn from the Alamosa cops and the state agents ended with a final round of dispirited questioning in my office.

I had gone over all this with Alicia. We had talked several times by telephone during the weeks since the murders in the valley. I was worried about her and warned her repeatedly to never be alone after work, to watch out for anyone following her. She was more worried about me and my mental state and had insisted several times that I cut down on my drinking. She had argued for me to take a long break, but so far that discussion had gone nowhere. I had eased up on the afternoon beers and quit substituting alcohol for dinner, and at least twice a week I threw on some old sweats and tennies and ran a few blocks through the neighborhood. It wasn't fun, it wasn't pretty and it hurt like hell, but I kept at it because Alicia had asked me to do it.

We nicknamed the murderous stranger from the valley "the Lexus guy" and although she joked about him and his careless-ness, I couldn't treat him as lightly. I told her to have the police watch out for her and she did convince a couple of her friends on the Pueblo force to cruise by her home and work place more than usual.

At the close of one of our conversations on a chilly October night, I said, "At least Tyler Boudin's disappeared. He hasn't popped up unexpectedly swinging his fists and steel-toed boots at Denver lawyers too drunk to defend themselves."

That, of course, jinxed it.

I said goodnight, finished some minor details in a few of my cases and left the office.

Midnight in the part of Denver the Chamber of Commerce types dubbed LoDo could be noisy and boisterous. Revelers whooped it up and pretended that Denver had a Mardi Gras season. Loud groups of young men and women congregated on every corner in LoDo, and cops slowly drove past, sometimes flashing a light in a surprised young lawyer's face or using a bullhorn to admonish an even younger banker. Similar scenes, but not as upscale, happened on East Colfax Avenue, West Thirty-Eighth Avenue, and the Five Points area.

Those same Chamber of Commerce types had been trying for a few years to tag a name on the area around my office, near the courthouse. They wanted to call it the Golden Triangle, but so far that appellation hadn't really stuck with the masses. During the day, traffic congested on the streets surrounding city hall. Lawyers, politicians, defendants, families of defendants—all trooped to the same building where their business had to be resolved. School kids teemed around the library and the art museum, and their yellow and black buses spewed exhaust while RTD buses honked and squeaked at the numerous intersections. A few restaurants, bars and art galleries dotted the remaining blocks, but mostly the area south of Colfax and West of Broadway was made up of small businesses like copy centers, collection agencies, bail bond outfits and the occasional law partnership or solo practitioner. My sign—Luis Móntez, Esq.—hung there. Rosa worked for me there, and I did all I could to keep both the sign and Rosa.

The Triangle could be a hectic, even invigorating metropolitan hub. A good place to make a living, if your living had anything to do with the tragedies or comedies that played out in the stuffy, airless Denver courtrooms.

But midnight—a different story altogether. The Triangle was quiet, dark, and menacing. The ominous main building of the Denver Police Department stood guard at the corner of Cherokee and Fourteenth but a few blocks away where I had to park my car a person could feel as vulnerable as a blind man lost in a strange city.

Tyler Boudin waited for me by my car. A creature of habit, I thought. This time I could see him before he had a chance to pounce, but it was obvious he wasn't hiding. He smoked a cigarette. He waved at me when he saw me stop a dozen yards from him. I reached inside my suit coat and pulled out the twenty-five year old 9mm Walther PPK I had begun to carry at night. The gun was a direct result of Boudin's last visit with me, the time he had stomped me in the parking lot of Gordon's Lounge. I aimed my weapon at him.

"Get away from my car, Boudin."

He dropped his cigarette and raised his arms.

"Let me explain, Móntez. No need for the piece."

I motioned him away from my car with the stubby barrel of the 9mm.

"Get the hell away from my car, and from me. Just leave and I won't have to use this."

"You know I'm an agent with the DEA. I got my shield right here in my pocket. I'm not trying to hurt you. I told you I can explain. Give me a chance."

"I'll give you a chance to get the hell out of here."

"Móntez, I'm sorry. You got no reason to believe me, but I had to do it. You were blowing my cover. You were putting us both in danger, man. I had to make it look like you had no connection to me. If I didn't make it look good, we both could have been hurt. We would have been dead, man."

In my hand the compact gun weighed as heavy as the darkness, felt as thick as the night.

"I get it. You beat me to save my ass. Thanks."

"Let me explain. Give me a chance. Five minutes, then I get out of your life forever if that's what you want. Five minutes."

Tyler Boudin appeared to be wearing some of the same clothes he had on the night he kicked in my ribs. His long, oily dark hair had been clumped together in a ponytail, and the black tee-shirt was covered with a leather jacket sporting the colors of one of Colorado's outlaw motorcycle clubs, the Iron Cowboys. His wiry beard shook with his words and his constant head movements.

I said, "I have no reason to believe anything you say. Why should I listen? Why shouldn't I put a bullet in your kneecap and leave you here like you left me? Why the hell should I even let a pig like you keep living?"

"Because of Alicia. Alicia Aragón. She's in danger, Móntez. And you need me to help her."

Midnight in downtown Denver could be filled with the sounds of drunken laughter against the brass of a salsa band providing rhythm for the night; the rush of traffic escaping the performing arts center complex after a late end to a touring New York play; the explosions and colors of a fireworks show over the baseball stadium.

Or midnight in Denver could be nothing more than the thump of a man's blood pumping through the wounded vessels of his heart, the humming in his ears caused by fear, the scuffle of a man's boots against a crack in the pavement.

I moved to within a few inches of Boudin's face. I pointed the gun at his throat.

I said, "If you . . ."

"Not me, asshole! I'm trying to tell you that she's in danger, but we can stop it. We can help her."

"What's your story, Boudin? You got those five minutes you wanted."

His body slumped, loosened up after the tension of the past few seconds. I jammed the barrel in his chest and he went rigid again.

"You stumbled into something big, Móntez. When you started fooling around with Mariele Castilla, and asking about me, and talking to assistant district attorneys, you opened up a fucking can of maggots. You got no idea. No fucking idea at all, do you?"

"I know about you, don't I? All I need to know. Narc gone bad. Racist dog using his badge to get away with all kinds of crap, including setting up Dominic Santos for a jailhouse hit and roughing me up so that I don't get too close to your play."

His contempt for me oozed from his pores. Even with a gun jammed against his muscles he had no fear of me. He must have felt that he was protected, secure behind his badge and his size. He relaxed again, lowered his defenses a notch or two.

Tyler Boudin towered over me and had a good forty pounds and at least fifteen years of an advantage. But the bone around my eye socket twitched and a sharp crease of pain shot through my cortex, a remembrance of the night he had smashed my face. My side ached, another memento. My brain flashed on him pounding me, on the words "Goddamn Mexicans" covered with his spit and hatred, and on the panic I had felt as I writhed on the asphalt, a target for his fists and boots.

There's a thin line between love and hate and, sometimes, there's only a shade of gray between reason and outrageous. It wasn't hard for me to filter through that border that night.

I swung at him with all my weight, both my hands gripping the gun, smashing it into his guts. I felt the give of his flesh, the surprise and anger that wanted to erupt from within his massive frame. He gasped and pitched forward and my knee met his face, causing a sound I had never heard before. He was on his knees, blood flowing from his nose. I put the gun to his ear.

"Start talking, motherfucker. Talk like your life depended on it. Talk before I change my mind and we both regret this night."

He groaned. He lifted his head, grabbed his nose and tried to stop the bleeding.

"You sonofabitch. You broke my nose."

"Not what I want to hear, Boudin. What the hell's going on?"

I thumped his skull with the gun. His head swayed backwards but he stayed on his knees.

He said, "Drugs . . . millions of dollars of drugs coming through the valley . . . uhh . . . been on the case for four years . . . Uhh . . . Dominic Santos was my in, the bag man . . . the guy who picked up and delivered the money."

His words were slow, surrounded with air. He slurped blood

while he talked. I nudged him on the ear to keep him talking. At any second he could reach up and take the gun away from me. I knew I would shoot him if he tried.

I said, "You went to prison to hook up with Dominic Santos?"

"Yeah . . . sure. The creep was a snitch in the New Mexico joint. It was easy getting him to think I could help him . . . . Uhh . . . . He gave me information about the Mexican gangs and I watched his back. We were the odd couple . . . but it worked."

"Then you tried to get to him again when he was in the Denver jail. And you killed him."

He jerked his head and blood sprayed on both of us.

"No, no! I went in the Denver jail because Dominic was ready to help me out . . . he knew I was a cop. He thought he could work out a deal . . . he was facing serious time on the arson but he knew I had more on him. The whole valley drug-smuggling business could be laid on him. He was desperate for a deal . . . ready to turn snitch again . . . . Uhh . . . . But when I got inside, someone had worked him against me, had him acting crazy, all stirred up. He started a fight . . . and then, in the mess of the riot . . . someone killed him. It wasn't me. I needed him. I wanted to get him out. But he wouldn't listen. Someone else killed him."

"Dominic set the fire at Barber's cabin?"

"I don't think so. Not his style. More like something Mariele would do. He wasn't really worried about that. He had bigger things on his mind . . . . Uhh, damn! Man, I need some help. The bleeding won't stop."

"Plenty of time for that. So what's this got to do with Alicia? Why did you drag her into this?"

He sat back on his haunches and pinched his nostrils together. He grimaced. His words were strained.

"I didn't. You did. When she showed up in the valley, I started hearing talk that she was your old lady . . . that you had been working for old man Santos and that crazy Mariele. Word got out that you and the Pueblo woman knew more than you told the cops about the killings . . . about Dominic . . . about all of it. And then, the people running the drug show, they must have got antsy, nervous about a Denver lawyer who acted stupid but who might know more than he let on. I was supposed to feel you out, see how much you really did know and either take care of you or make sure that you stayed stupid . . . and Alicia, she's supposed to be a warning to you, just in case. I got hired to kill her, Móntez."

"Hired by who? Who?"

I held my gun over his bleeding face.

He raised his hands to protect his wounded nose and the blood flowed like one of the *acequias* of water driving the valley war.

"The guy who worked the deals . . . made the connections to dealers around the country. He's as close as I got . . . but he's not the main guy. He's not the one we want. I was close to meeting the real money man, the boss, before all this happened, before the fire and Dominic's killing. Now . . ."

"Who is it, Boudin? Who's the guy who told you to kill Alicia Aragón?"

"He only passed on the word. Like I said, he's not the main guy."

"I don't care! The name!"

"Okay, okay! His name's Michael. Michael Torres."

I swung at him with the butt of the gun and I cracked the top of his head. The PPK was hard enough to hurt him but it was not heavy enough to inflict any real damage and I used it more like ballast for my fist than a club. He toppled on his side, groaning, twitching from the pain of the blow. I hit him again, and again, but what I was aiming at was the face of my nephew, the face of Michael Torres. I tried to erase Michael, to return him to the time when he was only my trouble-prone nephew, the relative who couldn't get a break. It worked. Boudin no longer was Michael. For an instant he had changed into Freddie Canales, an image that shocked me and brought me back. When I stopped, Tyler Boudin lay like a bundle of rags on the street. A bloody, soiled, useless bundle of rags.

"Stop! Drop your gun!"

I was surrounded by flashing red and white light. Before I had a chance to respond I was tackled and pinned to the street by a cop with coffee breath. I didn't struggle.

FIFTEEN

THE TWO COPS who saw me pistol-whipping Boudin had been witnesses against several of my clients and, although they had no love for me, they at least gave me professional deference. Anybody who still believes it's what you know and not who you know that matters, must live a very sheltered life. Coffee-breath was a veteran, Calhoun. Everything by the book, no chances taken and, therefore, nothing left to chance. The younger of the two was the only Native American on the force, and, as far as I knew, he could have been the only Indian cop in any big city police department. He was a dark-eyed, taupe-colored Navajo who called himself Ben Wayne Johnson. He always smiled when he said his name but I never understood the humor. Although he had been on the opposite side of some of my cases, we had no other history, no negative karma waiting to pounce, no skeletons rattling in any closets.

I wasn't booked, locked up, or otherwise mistreated. They did call for another car to take in Boudin, who had maintained consciousness but wasn't saying much. I assumed he ended up with a doctor. The cops had no interest in him, one way or the other.

Calhoun had a discreet talk with the Navajo, then he was gone. Ben Wayne Johnson went along with my request to speak with assistant district attorney Rolanda Alvarez. He parked me in an interrogation room with a cup of coffee without starting any of the formal processing required for an arrest. Boudin's blood spotted my suit coat.

Ben Wayne Johnson said, "We'll wait on the ADA. See what Alvarez wants to do."

I couldn't let myself believe what Tyler Boudin had told me. I had known Michael all of his life, had treated him like a son. There had been a time when he had been a wild one, and the scorpion-shaped scar across his left eyebrow attested to his tough life in the streets of Albuquerque as a boy. His mother Graciela— my sister—had not been strong, and when she finally succumbed to drugs and alcohol and bad men, Michael had left that part of the family and never looked back. That had been years before, and the Michael Torres I thought I knew would have had nothing to do with a threat against Alicia Aragón.

Michael was *familia*, part of the Móntez blood. There was just no way that Boudin had told me the truth.

I tried to explain all that to Rolanda Alvarez when she arrived at the cop station, hair in a loose clump on the top of her head, wearing a sweater over a pair of jeans, and rubbing the sleep out of her eyes.

"This guy Boudin tried to assault you? And he's done it before? Why didn't you file a complaint? I told you not to get involved with this guy. I told you it was a federal bag of worms, Louie. I'm not sure I can cover for you this time. Not sure I want to."

I loved this woman. She had to help me. I knew it, she knew it. But she had to talk tough about doing it and so for forty-five minutes I listened to her lectures and her warnings, and I even apologized somewhere in there, although I'm not sure for what. I did regret the way I had manipulated her in the first place and when I admitted that I had overstepped the line when I had played the secretary-on-the-side card she finally cut the sermonizing and arranged for me to go home.

"This all assumes that Tyler Boudin doesn't scream to my boss, Louie. He signs a complaint, goes to the press, anything like that, I can't help. The arresting officers are willing to allow that you could have been defending yourself, and as long as we got the gun there won't be any fuss made about your concealing that weapon. That's as far as we can go. Don't expect me to file a charge against Boudin."

"No, Rolanda, I don't expect anything like that. But, ¡cálmate! Tyler Boudin won't complain, won't breathe a word of what happened to anybody. It's part of his job. He's the last person on earth who wants it out that he got dropped by me. He doesn't even want it known that he was anywhere near me tonight."

"Then you better watch your ass. That guy can hurt you. Bad."

"Really? Thanks for the advice, Rolanda. Timely as all hell."

She rolled her red-streaked eyes and shook her head and clucked her teeth.

I had done it again. I just couldn't hold back when it came to chiding people like Rolanda or Harry López. Alicia would have charley-horsed my shoulder and told me to shut up.

"Okay, okay, truce. I mean it, Rolanda. You came out tonight when you didn't have to, and you kept my butt out of jail. Thank you."

She stared at me for a minute, waiting for the punch line, the dig that she had come to expect from me. When it didn't happen, she said, "I'll have some people check up on Michael Torres. And we'll get a warning to Ms Aragón. But I think you're right and the narc was just blowing smoke. Who knows what this Boudin's up to? Why did he even meet up with you?"

She thought over her words, looked me up and down and frowned.

She said, "I'll send a detective to interview him before the doctor releases him. Boudin's story doesn't click but we should run it down as much as we can. And I'm going to talk to the head of the Denver DEA office. Boudin needs to be brought in, tranquilized, or something. They hate it when one of us locals gets in their business, but that's the way it goes. Right, Louie?"

I lifted myself from the hard metal chair. I hesitated, not sure, feeling awkward. Then I reached out and hugged her. I thought Alicia would have appreciated that gesture. Rolanda was so surprised she walked out of the room without saying anything.

!!!

It was after four in the morning. The bars were closed, if I had been so inclined, and I didn't know if I should call Alicia, if I should confront Michael with Boudin's story, or if I should simply go home and try to sleep.

I walked from the cop station to my car, surrounded by the eerie quiet of a city that I didn't recognize, a quiet almost as complete as the pitch-black Colorado night I had found in the isolation of the San Luis Valley. The crisp autumn breeze had cleansed the air and above me the stars didn't have to struggle to break through leftover smog and dust and the heartbreak of the day.

A truck rumbled through a street that could have been one block over or on the other side of the skyline—I couldn't pinpoint the location and so the sound came from everywhere. The driver of the truck tried to change gears but he missed and the grinding noise echoed from one building to another.

I hunched my shoulders in a feeble attempt to keep out the wind, a harbinger of the winter that was well on its way.

The headlights blinded me before I knew what they were. I had carelessly walked into the parking lot when the darkness suddenly was split with piercing beams of light. I held up my hands to block out the glare but for several seconds my eyes saw only moving golden spots. I hadn't anticipated one surprise that night, I never could have guessed at two.

The voice said, "Móntez. Don't move, *hombre*. You're dead if you do."

I recognized Emilio's tone. I figured that the headlights came from his Lexus and that he held a Desert Eagle in his hand, aimed at my head. I raised my arms and tried to inch around the beams so that I could see.

"I said don't move, Móntez. Stay right there."

The truck with the groaning transmission rounded the corner. The driver tried to downshift and again he ground the gears. The truck's headlights lit up the area around all of us. I ignored Emilio's order and moved an inch to my right. Emilio stood next to his car and another man stood next to him but it all happened so fast that I didn't get a good look at the second man, other than to know that he was there. They turned and looked at the truck in the street only a few yards from them. The driver honked his horn. The two men dropped to their knees, trying to stay out of the driver's vision. I ran the few feet to my car, clicked the button on my key to unlock the door and jumped in. The truck had stopped in the street and the driver had stepped down.

"Hey! What the hell's going on? What is this?"

Emilio aimed his gun at the truck driver.

"Leave, mister. Now! This ain't none of your business."

"What the. . .? You got a gun? Goddamn, nobody draws a gun on me. You better use it, buddy, 'cause I got one, too."

Someone fired off a shot. The truck driver fell to the ground. He held a huge gun, something like an old Colt .45. He aimed and shot at Emilio's car. Emilio and his friend scrambled to the far side of the Lexus. The truck driver ran back to his truck and slammed the cab door behind him. Another shot rang out. The truck lumbered away with the transmission screaming in protest and the engine pouring smoke in its wake.

I started my car and squealed out of the parking lot. My rear window shattered and I heard the bullet bury itself in the interior roof of my car. I headed for the police station that I had left only a few minutes before. Cops were streaming from the building. I stopped and jumped out, my hands above my head again. Officer Ben Wayne Johnson grabbed me.

"You live way too much in the fast lane, *amigo*."

I answered him as calmly as I could. The words came out in shouts.

"Two guys just tried to kill me! Back by my car!"

"That is one busy parking lot tonight."

My ex sister-in-law's sweaty, agitated face intruded on the Navajo and me.

"Jesus Christ, Louie! Jesus Christ!"

!¦¦

It was close to dawn when I left the police station for the second time that night. Rolanda had advised me to stay in a motel for a day or two, just in case. Instead, I asked that the cops drive by my place periodically, and she set it up for me.

Ben Wayne Johnson escorted me to my car. No one waited in the shadows, no one pulled a gun, no one threatened me.

Johnson had carried a roll of duct tape from the station house and I pulled out the cardboard sun shade from the trunk. We used the shade for a patch on the shot-out rear window.

Johnson said, "For tonight, it'll do. Tomorrow's a different story."

I eased myself into the front seat. "Always is. Thanks for the help."

The cop shut the door for me. He stood tall next to my car and looked around the lot.

"I think it's clear, Móntez. No strange Lexus in the shadows. You sure you don't want one of us to follow you home? Or we could put you up in a special cell we got for guys like you. Guys who seem to be on everybody's hot list. What do you say?"

He stood in darkness and I didn't look too hard or long at him so the details of his face were a mystery, but I assumed he was smiling as he talked. I hoped he was smiling.

"Thanks, but no thanks. A squad car driving by every hour or so should make my neighbors' paranoia light up like the Christmas lights they like to hang. That should be enough."

"Okay, counselor. By the way, if I were you, I wouldn't use that parking lot anymore."

"Have to. I'm paid up for the rest of the month."

I headed home to make a few telephone calls, and for some sleep.

I was tired. Tired of getting ambushed in parking lots. Tired of being chased through the countryside. Tired of looking over my shoulder for a white man with a big hate, or a brown man with a big gun. Tired of not knowing why I had become a target, why Mariele and old man Santos had been killed, why Alicia was in danger just because she took me in one night like a child might take in a bird with a broken wing.

The phone was ringing as I walked in the house.

"Hello? What is it?"

"Móntez? It's me. Emilio. You're one lucky bastard, dude. But, I ain't that easy to get rid of. You have to see me tonight.

Or, this morning, I guess it is. I'll come by and pick you up. No cops, of course."

"You're either sick or stupid."

"Easy, *ese*. Your girlfriend . . . *¿cómo se llama?* Alicia? She's lonely here, bud. Needs some company. I think you should be polite and pay her a visit. Okay?"

He moved his phone. I heard Alicia's voice.

"I'm okay. They're . . ."

There was a loud thud, and the sounds of people moving quickly, and of a phone yanked from Alicia's hands.

Emilio came back on the line.

"*¡Qué mujer!* Stubborn. You got your hands full there, man. Anyway, I'll be by in twenty minutes. You be waiting outside your house. And if there's any sign of cops, or anything that even smells like a cop, your friend has a really unpleasant time ahead of her. *¿Me entiendes?*"

"You do anything to her and I'll kill you! Do you understand *that?*"

"You may have your chance, dude. Someone has to die. That's what this is all about, no?"

SIXTEEN

NINETEEN MINUTES LATER, Emilio drove up to the curb in front of my house, where I waited. I opened the passenger door and sat in a worn but soft leather seat. He had on the same hat—Los Lobos—and a black leather overcoat over a pair of jeans and a black turtleneck. The barrel of his gun poked out from between his legs in an obscene gesture of contempt for me and what I could do to him. A song with accordion and guitar and very sad lyrics played in the background. Eventually, I recognized it as "*Mi Ranchito*," the version recorded by Los Super Seven.

He glanced at me and said, "You're a hard man to pin down."

"What is this about? What do you think you want with me?"

"Let's wait to talk about that when we get someplace where I can keep my eye on you. *¿Está bien?*"

"Where's your buddy?" Something like a smile creased his *indio* face. "There were two of you in Pueblo, and the valley, and the parking lot. You working alone now?"

"You're a nosy guy, Móntez. All things come to those who wait. *Paciencia, hombre*. Life's too short as it is. I've seen it end suddenly, bro. Usually to men who are in an awful hurry to get to that end, until they finally make it."

The sun kicked into the sky behind us. "He's with Alicia. Sonofabitch."

He smiled again but said nothing in response. He drove quietly, efficiently, out of my neighborhood and north on Zuni until he reached Forty-Sixth Avenue. West to Federal, north again to the Interstate, then west again. Traffic had started to build but it was nowhere near what it would be in another hour, and he made good time. During the uneventful ride neither of us spoke. The CD moved on and Los Super Seven played through until they finished with a sentimental accordion riff by Flaco Jiménez. At Lowell he exited again and drove a few blocks north to a modest frame house.

The music stopped abruptly and Emilio parked the car.

He followed me up the walk. The place was in good shape, paint kept up, neat yard, no trash. It could have been a nice home for a working family, or a comfortable deal for a group of Regis University students, or a cover for a con man. I recognized the house and I knew who waited in it with Alicia.

The thick wooden door opened and then the black iron security door swung outward to admit us.

Before I saw him, I said, "Harry, I'll kill you if Alicia's hurt!"

Unintelligible swearing filtered through the room. Emilio pushed me from behind with what felt like the barrel of his gun and I continued walking. We passed through the large living room. The details jumped out at me but I denied them in an attempt to convince myself that I was wrong, that I had never been in that house before, that I had never met a client in that room, sat near the gas fireplace talking about Harry's court appearance, going over the possible sentence, weighing the DA's offer. The cheap couch dressed up with a Mexican blanket that had halfway slipped onto the gray, wooden floor; the painting by a local Chicano artist who admired Frida Kahlo and included marigolds in all of his work; and something new, a picture in a somber, olive green frame with a dull brown matte— a picture of a young, smiling Freddie Canales, before prison. We walked into a bright yellow kitchen with a yellow refrigerator and a white round table with white chairs. Alicia sat in one of the chairs, her hands tied around the back of the chair.

I tried to rush to her but Emilio got in my way and waved me to another chair with his gun. Harry López appeared from a corner and flipped rope around my arms and quickly and expertly tied me up.

Harry said, "Okay, everything's copasetic now. Finally."

"I'm going to break you in half, Harry. What the hell do you think you're doing?"

His smile was brighter than the gleam from the refrigerator. I looked away, to Alicia.

"Are you all right?"

She nodded and tried to give me a reassuring smile. It didn't work.

She said, "The Lexus guy."

I looked directly at Harry. "If you've done anything to her your miserable life is over."

Harry quit smiling. He reached behind himself and produced a gun, another large caliber killing tool, blue-black and heavy.

"I've put up with a lot of shit from you, Móntez. Now, the worm has turned, don't you think, dog? High and mighty lawyer who couldn't win a big case if he was fucking the judge. Your worthless ass belongs to me. I can do whatever the hell I want with you, or your girlfriend, and you can't do a damn thing about it."

To prove his point he slapped my face. My head whipped backwards but the slap barely stung me. He hadn't used the gun, and he wasn't as big as Tyler Boudin, so I didn't feel like I really had been hit. And he hadn't turned Emilio loose on me.

López must not have enjoyed hitting me. He didn't do it again. He said, "Your girlfriend was good insurance. Got you here in no time. You were very lucky downtown. If that damn trucker hadn't interfered, well . . ."

Alicia said, "What happened?"

I answered since neither Harry or Emilio appeared eager to fill her in on the details.

"They tried to ambush me at my car. Lucky for me a good Samaritan saw these jerks and spoiled their fun."

She frowned. "When they were gone, just a while back. So you wouldn't be here except that they got me? I'm sorry."

"Hell with that, Alicia. You got nothing to be sorry about. It's this creep, Harry López. Soon as he tells me what this is about, maybe we can clear it up and get out of here."

Emilio rubbed his chin. Harry said, "I wish it was that easy, Móntez. But it's not. Complicated, actually."

Alicia looked strung out and on the edge of losing whatever self-control had stayed with her through the night so far. I forced myself to deal with Harry in a way that I hoped would help her.

I said, "I'm not going anywhere, Harry. You've got a captive audience."

Emilio laughed and Harry grinned like somebody had wired his jaw open.

"You're a card, dickhead," Harry blurted. "Always liked that about you. What I *don't* like about you is that you're just another rip-off, a sellout, like so many other so-called Chicano lawyers. Sell your own people out, just for a buck."

The guy telling me this unexpected news was the guy who had swindled old ladies—old Mexican ladies—out of savings accounts that had been funded by their dead husbands' Black Lung benefits or railroad pension checks. Harry had convinced the *señoras* that he had located long lost, and rich, relatives from south of the border who only needed some "up-front American money" to get in the country, where they would share their Mexican wealth, after it had been converted to gringo greenbacks, of course.

"Yeah, yeah. I'm just a *vendido*, Harry. A money-grubbing stooge for the system. But I'm the guy you came to when you needed help. You slimy pig."

"That's another thing I like about you, dog. Your vocabulary. Once in a while you throw out some ten-dollar words. Good show for your cop pals, or the judges. But, you know what? It don't fit. Education doesn't sit well on you, Móntez. You're a bottom dweller like me. Only difference, I never sent no poor kid to the pen just because I got bought off. Only you can do that, Móntez. Only you and your education. Only you are that low."

Alicia spit out her words. "What are you saying? Luis has done more for you and people like you than practically anybody else in this town. He's kept you *out* of prison! You're talking crazy." Rage and tension colored her speech.

Emilio was wrapped up in the small drama in front of him. The careless hit man had let his grip on his gun slip a bit, and the way it dangled from his fingers reminded me of a small boy twirling his pop gun in a juvenile display of gun showmanship. A small boy can be surprised, outsmarted. But I was securely tied to my chair and Alicia was in the line of any fire the two whack jobs might get off.

I said, "He's talking about Freddie Canales, Alicia. He thinks I sold him out."

Alicia shook her body as though the ropes were water and she could make them drop just by moving.

Harry stood up. "*Orale*. This guy finally figured it out. What do you think about that Emilio? Didn't I tell you?"

Emilio's words were slow to come out, but they hit hard. "Hard to believe, man. Móntez had a rep in the hood. You did some good things, bud. When you were just a college kid, standing up for your *gente*. Then, the cases you handled, the stands you took. I'm really disappointed, brother. Sad, even."

He twirled his gun in the palm of his hand and aimed it at me. His grip was sure and steady and his eyes were bright and alive with the thought that he would do what we all expected of him and he would do it well and successfully. With that simple, small gesture, my respect for the man increased a hundredfold.

I said, "Just because this jerk says something doesn't make it so. I don't know why he even cares about Freddie Canales, but I did everything I could to keep that kid out of jail. It was a tough loss for me . . ."

Harry exploded. "For you! You motherfucker! Freddie was the greatest! He was going to be somebody! He had talent, he was an artist! If you had just done your damn job, he would have walked. He never would have been sent to that fucking hole! You killed him as much as those cops, Móntez. You killed my boy. My son. And now, I'm going to kill you. We should have smoked you in Alamosa. No one stops me now!"

It can be that way. We all know it. We've all whistled that song about the ancient idea that it's a small world. My closet-sized existence and Harry's tiny universe had just collided.

"Your son? Freddie Canales was your kid? Why . . . why didn't you ever tell me, Harry? Why didn't you help during the trial? Why keep it a secret?"

Emilio whispered his words. "Easy there, brother. You know how these things are. Harry and Freddie's mama had a Mrs. Jones thing going, you know? She never told Freddie or her old man about Harry's, uh, relationship to the family. Dig it, you know Pete Canales. Even I heard about that man. Mean as a rabid dog and more crazy. *Olvídate.* Both Mrs. Canales and Harry would have been sliced up into little, bitty *pedacitos. Pendejo* Harry was lucky he got away with what he did. He's not exactly the smartest guy running around the neighborhood, but he is the luckiest."

My mouth must have been hanging open with my tongue scraping Harry's waxed floor. I had a very hard time believing that Harry had cuckolded Pete Canales, and was still alive. But, there it was.

Harry slumped back in his chair. "I loved that kid. I did what I could for him, through his mother. Money, clothes, little things when we could get away with it and Margaret had a good cover. I was saving money for him to go to school. But it all ended. Because of you. The kid was defending himself, for Christ sake! You were paid off to blow his case, to go through the motions and nothing else."

He straightened himself and raised his gun in my direction.

Alicia whimpered. "Don't, please. Don't hurt him. It wasn't his fault."

I answered as slowly as I could. "Harry, I don't know where you got that idea. But it didn't go down that way. No one paid me off. Why would they? Who would have done that? Freddie wasn't that important."

Harry's red face twisted crazily.

"Not important! You sorry-assed punk! Joey Rodríguez got to you! Everyone knew it. You can't talk your way out of this one."

He was wrong, of course. I had never accepted a bribe in my life. A bribe had never been offered to me. Harry had created a story about Rodríguez and Freddie and me, and there wasn't anything I could say to change that story.

Emilio moved in his chair, distracting all of us. He rested his huge, ludicrous Magnum on the white table. He pulled a smaller gun from inside his leather coat. It could have been a short-barrel .22.

That's when Harry's famous luck ran out.

The bullet from Emilio's gun tore through Harry's right eye and smashed him against his chair. He didn't fall over. His remaining eye focused on Emilio until it clouded over and his body slumped.

My brain was useless, in shock. Alicia cringed and fell to the floor, the chair twisting around her back.

Emilio was saying something. His words slowly made their way into my understanding.

". . . *pendejo*, always a *pendejo*. Guy just never wised up."

He walked over to Alicia and I strained madly against the ropes that held my wrists. Emilio helped her sit up. He said, "You want some water or something?" She shook her head. "*¿Nada?* Okay."

He left the room for a few seconds and returned with a large canvas bag. He dumped Harry into the bag. Then he painstakingly cleaned up the killing area. He mopped, used rags from under the sink, wiped down the chair. There wasn't much blood—the small caliber bullet had guaranteed that, but Emilio was thorough. He picked up Harry's gun from the floor and set it on the counter near the sink. He used Harry's cleaning materials and had the kitchen back to its usual pristine condition in less than half an hour.

Alicia and I could only watch and wait. He was quick and quiet, so much more in control than either Alicia or I. Every few minutes her body shook with stifled sobs.

Finally, Emilio threw his cleaning tools in the bag with Harry.

"I got to go."

He looked at me.

"We all got motives, Móntez. Even you, bud. You forget all about me, and I'll be mutual. I figure you owe me anyway. I wasn't sure what was going to play out tonight, not until just a few minutes ago. I could tell Harry was talking crazy. Joey Rodríguez didn't have the smarts to get to Freddie's lawyer. And for what? Just so he could get back at him in prison? Who thinks like that? Only Harry. *Pendejo* Harry."

Alicia sobbed. Emilio frowned, then said, "It's okay. May not seem like it, but it is. Harry was going to do to you what I just did to him. Except, he would have been a lot messier, don't you think? Look at that piece of iron he was going to use on you." He nodded in the direction of the counter. "So, let's keep this between us, okay? *Pero*, you should get out pretty quick before you have to explain what the hell you're doing here. Your stories are probably starting to sound a little suspicious to the cops, no?"

I wanted to come back with a smart answer, something glib and cute. But the gray canvas bag and its terrible load had me paralyzed.

Emilio, on the other hand, appeared to be liberated. He had found his voice.

"I'll tell you this. Harry's the one that got Mariele and old man Santos to hire you for Dominic. He was setting you up back then and he used them to get you to the valley. I think she was in on it, too, but I couldn't tell you why exactly. They must have been in together on a con of the old man. They sure wanted me to do you in the valley. I strung them along, made excuses. But, then, that's where it went haywire. When Mariele and Santos turned up dead, López didn't know what to think, what to do. Lucky for you, *ese*. Made Harry think he had to back off and take care of you here in the city, where he felt safe. Guess he was wrong, *ey*?"

I said, "What about Tyler Boudin? What's he got to do with you?"

As he untied Alicia's ropes he said, "Ee-hoe-lay, man. Only Mariele could have told you anything about that sonofabitch. And she's long gone, bro."

The ropes fell from Alicia's wrists. She rubbed them, trying to get the blood back.

Emilio turned his blue-black eyes on me. "I know where you live and work and get drunk and where your father lives and even where you buy your groceries. And, I know where she lives." He pointed at Alicia. "You remember that. "

He picked up Harry's gun, dropped it in a pocket of his overcoat, humped the bag over his shoulder, and walked out the back door. We heard the Lexus start up and drive away. Except for the smell of death that stuck in my nostrils nothing remained from the shooting.

SEVENTEEN

"WHAT JUST HAPPENED? Why did he do that? And in front of witnesses?"

I thought out loud, rambled an explanation for her that I made up as I talked.

"Harry thought Emilio was working for him, but that turned out to be Harry's big mistake. Emilio has another boss. Harry worked hard to set me up. He wanted me in the valley, and he got me there. My death could have been blamed on the water war. There would have been many suspects. Mariele, Barber, Boudin. They all could catch heat for killing me, maybe because I was too nosy, or in the way. Harry conned Santos into hiring me to represent Dominic, knowing that sooner or later I would have to go to the valley to work on Dominic's case. Dominic's death in the county jail moved up the timetable, probably made Harry act faster than he had anticipated, made him rely on professional help for something he wanted to do himself."

Alicia finished untying the ropes around my wrists. I mimicked her and rubbed my wrists to get the blood flowing, to assure myself that I was still alive.

We talked about calling the police and waiting in Harry's house, but our hearts didn't back up our words. Emilio was long gone, and we believed that he knew how to cover his tracks and disappear. We didn't need to say that Emilio could return after he realized he had been too generous and he decided to clip the loose ends.

We left Harry's house and hoped none of his neighbors noticed us. How long would it take before Harry's absence would attract official attention? Would any of his friends miss him? Would some mark he had been working on take the extra step and make a phone call to report that Harry López had vanished?

At a convenience store I telephoned Rosa, caught her as she was leaving for the office and asked her to pick us up.

We waited in the store and the clerk must have thought we were ready to hold him up. Both of us looked like escapees from some type of institution. Our clothes were wrinkled and stale. Dark patches hung beneath Alicia's eyes and I assumed mine looked the same. We were edgy, drank a lot of the store's bad coffee, and stayed much too long leafing through the weight-lifting and teen celebrity magazines.

Rosa's arrival saved us from the clerk's accusatory glares. He must have been ready to call someone to come and get rid of us. We rushed outside to meet Rosa and climbed in her maroon three-year old Geo Tracker before she had a chance to turn off the engine.

"Louie? What happened?"

"Get us to the office and I'll tell it to you on the way. By the way, Rosa, meet Alicia, the person you've talked to on the phone. Alicia, this is Rosa, my secretary."

∷

Alicia filled a glass with water from the office cooler. Before she took a drink she said, "When Mariele and Mr. Santos were killed, it spooked Harry. He came back to Denver and decided to bide his time. What was all that in the valley, the following you around, the visit from Emilio?"

"I think that was Emilio. He was probably stalling Harry, trying to learn all that he could about Harry's plan, picking his time to do his own work. Then, he heard that I knew about him, that I wanted to talk to him, so that must have made him nervous. He held off Harry because he is a very careful man, contrary to first impressions."

She nodded. "Mariele knew him, talked to him, tried to get you to talk to him. That had to seem awfully weird to Emilio. And Mariele either knew Emilio through Harry, or vice versa. Harry was the one who connected Mariele and Santos to you."

I helped myself to water and thought only fleetingly about the bottle of scotch in the bottom drawer of my desk.

"Maybe old man Santos did hire Emilio. Maybe that's who he was working for all the time. But that still doesn't explain killing Harry. Or who killed Fermín Santos and Mariele Castilla."

Rosa stood in the doorway, her eyes wide and nervous. She frowned under her hairdo of green and blue streaks. "We better call the police."

"First, I'm calling my ex sister-in-law. She's going to love hearing from me again. And I know a cop who should be interested in all of this."

Alicia held me around the waist, half-asleep. Emilio and Harry had dragged her from her house the night before in a terrifying raid. They had waited for her to show up after work and were on her before she or the dogs could do anything. They had used a handkerchief soaked in some drug that had knocked her out. On the trip to Denver from Pueblo, she came to and while she was trussed and immobilized on the back seat of Emilio's car, she had expected to die. She realized that they were using her to get to me when Emilio had left her and Harry in Harry's kitchen, and the pitiful con man had said every crude and ugly thing he could about me and my representation of his doomed son, Freddie Canales.

She had tried to reason with him but he had long ago lost his patience for that virtue. He told her the day of Freddie's funeral was the day he had decided that I needed to die, too. I had been at that funeral. Harry was nowhere in sight that day. Whatever misguided notion he had about being a father had driven him to concoct a crazy scheme meant to end with my death, and the implication of people involved in their own nasty battles over water, power and money.

But that explained only some of it.

Rosa said, "I'll cancel your appointments. Can't see how you can work today." She was interrupted by the telephone ringing. She went to answer it, leaving Alicia and I to realize just how tired we were.

Alicia released her hold on me and walked away. It was a small gesture, nothing out of the ordinary, something that lovers do every day and I tried not to put the spin on it that could tear up my insides.

She stared at a row of law books in my bookcase, pretending that she might consider reading one of them. I finished off my water and waited. I knew that I should tell her about Tyler Boudin and his story about Michael Torres, and the threat to her life. But it was too much for me and I stepped back. I couldn't pile anything more on her.

Finally, she turned and said, "Is your life always this crazy?"

I started to laugh but the serious look on her face stopped me.

"I live a very boring life, actually. I do my work for my clients, visit my father, talk on the phone with my boys, pay my bills, and up until just recently I'd manage to do some drinking. And I thought I would be spending more time with you."

"Is that what you want?"

"Yes, Alicia. I would like that. If you let me."

Her eyes were half-closed. The struggle within her played out on her face. When the struggle stopped, it was obvious that she was close to telling me that I was more than she had bargained for, that being kidnapped and threatened had not been in her plans the night she took me to her house. What I saw on her face took me by surprise because all along I had thought that she was more durable than I, and that if there had to be a graceless end, I would be the one, again, who would bail out of the relationship.

"I don't know, Móntez. Last night, was . . . it was just too much. I need . . . some time. I'm tired, afraid. I went to the valley because I care for you. I wanted to help. But . . . seeing that man killed like that, and believing that we were going to be killed, too . . . . I'm not that strong. I haven't been a strong person for a long time."

I slammed my fist on my desk and she cringed.

"López!" He had hurt me in a way he could never imagine.

"I'm sorry. Just give me some time. Really, I'm sorry."

My throat swelled up and I couldn't speak. I wasn't sure what to say. I had been trained to think on my feet, to be ready to respond in the courtroom when I got an unexpected answer from a witness, to fake that the judge's question had not caught me completely by surprise. But right then, when I needed to speak and say something to this woman if I wanted her to stay in my life, my tongue stiffened and my heart grabbed any words I might have said and held them like they were the last pint of blood in my body.

She left the room and joined Rosa at her desk. I heard her ask about the bus station and about borrowing some money and about getting a cab. I stayed in my office while she and Rosa talked.

Rosa came to me. She said, "I'm taking Alicia to the bus station. I'll be back as soon as I can. You should call the district attorney, or the police. Alicia doesn't want to deal with any of this now. None of it."

The "none of it" had to include me.

Rosa made a production out of retrieving her keys from her purse. She asked, "You okay, Louie? You going to be all right?"

The power of speech returned but all I could whisper were glib, meaningless phrases.

"What can I say, Rosa? I'm alive, even though I had two killers point their guns at me last night. I'm alive even though I tangled with a brute, dirty federal cop. I'm alive. Got to be enough, I guess."

Alicia left without saying anything more to me.

I hadn't slept, hadn't eaten, still wore clothes stained with nervous sweat from my encounter with Harry López and drops of Tyler Boudin's blood. If my heart wasn't broken it was cracked in a crucial way. Without taking anything with me or locking any doors, I walked out of the office and headed in the direction of the Cherokee Grill.

An October rain fell on me. Light and misty with traces of snow, the shower was enough to produce rivulets of moisture that ran down my face like tears. My hair and the shoulders of my suit coat soaked through.

I imagined that Rosa's bright box of a vehicle would squeal up to me as I crossed the street and that Alicia would run to me and hug me and say that it was going to be all right, that she had recovered her senses, that she wanted to spend time with a broken-down lawyer who didn't want to be a lawyer anymore, who didn't know what he wanted to be now that he was forced to grow up, who had disrupted her calm, prosaic life of caring for her dogs and mourning her dead family. Why shouldn't she want to be with me?

I entered the Grill, ignored the hostess who asked me if I wanted "smoking or non-smoking," and sat at the bar. I perused the breakfast menu handed to me by the bartender.

"Scotch."

I kidded myself that I needed the drink to warm up. The bartender shrugged his shoulders but he poured my drink without comment.

A chill had settled in my back and my feet felt damp and cold. I rubbed a hand through my hair and shook out some rain.

I stared at the drink for a long minute before I took a sip. It tasted good, warmed me. I must have made a strange noise, or maybe it was just my general appearance, because the bartender intently watched me over the rim of a glass he feverishly polished with a bar rag.

I reeled from the bar stool and ran to the restroom. I hung over a toilet, my body heaving but nothing came out of me except the low wail of a man lost in a landscape he couldn't see. For five minutes my racked body shook and sweated.

When I calmed down I splashed water on my face, washed my hands, ran my pocket comb through my hair and breathed like a man rescued from drowning. I stared at myself in a mirror and vaguely recognized the bleary-eyed, yellow-skinned caricature that stared back. My clothes carried the odor of wet wool, dried blood, and perspiration.

The bartender stared as I walked past the bar. He said, "Hey, pal. I cleaned up your drink. I thought you were gone. Want another?"

There were a few customers sitting in booths eating

omelettes and pancakes, talking about the business of the coming day or the affairs of the previous night. They carried on and pretended that less than a dozen feet away, precariously leaning on the bar, there wasn't a strange, wild-looking Chicano who was ready to collapse.

"No thanks. I've had enough."

Part Four

The Flea and The Rat

✝

EIGHTEEN

GRACIELA HAD RESEMBLED her siblings only slightly but it was enough for all of us to be certain that we carried the same genes. Michael Torres had my sister's high cheekbones and heavy-lidded eyes and he looked a little like me even though he was *güero* and I was *prieto*. On certain days he could have been a younger version of me, if I wore cowboy boots and thick sheep-herder's vests.

Michael had been nervous since he had walked into my place of business. He tried to ease the tension with small talk and weak jokes.

"*Tío*, you're the Jessica Fletcher of Chicano lawyers. People die around you like you were a rat carrying the plague."

"It wasn't the rat, Michael. It was the flea on the rat that killed all those folks in the dark ages."

"Yeah, whatever, Louie. Mariele and Fermín. Dominic Santos. Then that Harry López. A regular epidemic. Can't blame Kyle Alarid on you. The fire that burned him was set before you got involved in all this. But still. And then last week? All that stuff coming down in one night. I hope *I'm* safe being here."

He was in my office because I had spent more than an hour on the phone that morning giving him the details about the message Tyler Boudin had delivered to me. At first, Michael tried laugh it off but when he heard the entire story, including the part about the end of Harry López, he insisted that he wanted to help me get to the truth. He traveled north to Denver and I met with him in my office as soon as he hit town.

A week had passed since Emilio had killed Harry. Seven days since Alicia had rushed back to Pueblo. I hadn't heard from either one of them. Tyler Boudin had pulled his vanishing act again. Rolanda had sent a message that she had to talk to me about that guy but she was in the middle of a first-degree murder trial and I had to wait my turn.

That left Michael Torres.

"On my way back I'll stop in Pueblo," he offered, "and talk with Alicia. She can't believe that I would have anything to do with trying to hurt her. Boudin's a nut case. He was out of control when he worked for Barber. And he was a cop all along! I saw him parade around the valley like a storm trooper. Nothing would surprise me about him. But why would he tell you that I wanted Alicia dead? And that I'm involved in selling drugs? I've heard some wild stories over the years, but that caps it."

It was one of those times when I had to put up or shut up. My sister's son was telling me that I had to reinforce the ties of blood that had bound us since he had been a child. I had relied on him and he had looked up to me, or so I had thought for many years. Could he really be a drug-dealing gangster who had ordered Alicia's death? To bite into that one I had to choose Boudin over Michael. The events of the past several weeks had me thinking long and hard about my choice, had me on the edge of succumbing to the darkest cynicism.

But this was *familia*, and I had to trust somebody.

There had been a time, during my first marriage, when Michael had lived in my house. For one summer he grew up with my sons as the country cousin who needed a break from his alcoholic mother and her string of boyfriends. He was the tough, anxious kid who learned to love baseball and the four of us attended several minor league games in old Mile High Stadium. We cheered the Zephyrs, ate hot dogs and drank sodas like any other extended family spending a day at the ballpark. We talked about the greats of the game—Willie Mays, Hank Aaron, Mickey Mantle, Roberto Clemente, Ty Cobb.

Michael always wanted to know more. He asked questions

that my sons didn't even think of, much less express. I told him what I knew and he found out more on his own so that by the end of the summer he was telling us details about these men. He knew that Mays and Aaron had both done quick tours through the Negro Leagues before they hit the big show. He filled us in on the details of Clemente's last plane trip, his mission of mercy that ended in his death. He knew that Cobb may have been the best hitter of all time but he also was the most hated man in baseball and when he asked me why I took the opportunity to expound on racism, sportsmanship, and the clay feet of manufactured heroes. Michael had been the kind of boy who would listen to such things. He listened and he remembered.

"Michael, I don't believe it. And I doubt that Alicia would believe it either. But . . . she reacted pretty strongly to everything that happened last week. I never spoke to her about what Boudin told me. It would've just added another layer of dirt on an already muddy picture. The way she feels now . . . she may not want to talk with you."

He sat upright and leaned forward. His voice was very serious when he said, "The man behind all of this has to be Matthew Barber. He's got the money, the connections, and he can be ruthless, Louie. I've seen him do things in the valley that you wouldn't think a quiet little white guy like that would even have kicking around in his head."

"But he's won, Michael. He beat the court case old man Santos had filed. No reason to kill him for that. The old man was finished. One of his lawyers told me as much, and when his son was killed, that finally ended it for him. He was ready to give up. Barber had nothing to fear from him anymore."

Michael nodded, and added, "And there doesn't seem to be a reason for Barber to put a hit on Harry López, or threaten Alicia. I guess Barber doesn't fit anywhere. So, what does that get you, Louie?"

"Tyler Boudin."

Michael had a hard time looking me in the eyes. His words were slow and exact. "Boudin lied about me. You do understand that?"

"I've already moved past that, Michael. Doesn't mean I

understand any of this." I paused. If he had any doubts about my reassurance, it was time for him to speak up. He waited for me. "What's your take?"

Michael took a deep breath. "Well, Boudin said he came after you in Pueblo because he was afraid you would blow his cover, and then he tried to create something between you and me when you whomped on him. He was still trying to set you up. And me. There's more?"

"Has to be, Michael. His undercover routine to ferret out the so-called big drug operation only gets him so far. He had to have been nervous when I asked around about him and Dominic. I talked with Rolanda Alvarez and eventually Boudin hears all about that. Then, after Santos and Castilla were killed, he pulled you out of a hat when I wanted more from him and I wasn't willing to go along with his BS. You were convenient. He knew you, and he knew I would probably overreact if I thought Alicia was in trouble."

Michael couldn't help grinning as he said, "He just didn't consider that you might overreact on him."

I rubbed my temples and sighed. "If I don't want to keep bumping into guys like Tyler Boudin and Emilio in parking lots, I have to put a stop to this. I've got to get to Boudin. I'd rather not meet up with Emilio again. There's nothing that connects them except me, and the Santos family apparently. Something to do with that family, or what used to be a family."

"Those are *two* guys you should stay away from, *tío*. Boudin's got to be pissed. And you know what that crazy Emilio can do. Why not take a vacation, a long one? Get out of town, lay low, and that could be it. Maybe it'll all blow over and you can get back to your normal life, your regular routine."

I wasn't comforted by that suggestion. Returning to normal didn't strike me as a viable option right then.

But I said, "Maybe, Michael. Maybe that is the way to go."

!!i

Before Michael left we gave each other an *abrazo* and several pats on the back. He assured me that he would stop in Pueblo and talk with Alicia. I asked him to tell her hello for me. He also said that he would see if he could come up with anything on Matthew Barber and his ties to Boudin or Emilio. He had already explained that Barber and Mariele Castilla had enjoyed a short-lived fling, but that appeared to be a pattern that she had repeated with several men in the valley. Then he was gone and from all appearances we were back on track as uncle and nephew. We had handcrafted an uneasy truce out of nothing more than bloodlines and distant, dim memories. It was a truce that could fall apart unless we were both strong, unless somewhere between us we found the truth.

⠇⠇⠊

Rosa helped me dig up all my old files on Harry López. Some of them had been buried in our storage room in the office's basement while others were only a few feet away in the current and active file cabinet.

Rosa had a few comments. "Burn it all. That guy was the devil and he's in hell now. Keeping this stuff can only bring bad luck."

I learned something very quickly from my review of Harry's files. I had underestimated how much he owed me. It was closer to three thousand than two, but it was all irrelevant, anyway. My bill had never been paid and now all it looked like I would get from Harry would be a tax write-off for a bad debt. The IRS people would never know just how bad that debt had been.

Funny how some of my best work brought up huge guilt pangs. I had saved Harry's ass several times. Cut him deals, finagled probation for him, copped him to minor charges when he should have been ridden hard by the system. That's what I do, I told myself. Better that a hundred guilty men go free than one innocent person do time—the standard defense attorney slogan. I wondered who represented those innocent persons, and I wondered if that attorney appreciated the job I did, if he or she understood the balance I helped maintain, if he or she saw how I made it all work. Yeah, right.

I used up most of the afternoon poring over Harry's life—at least the life that was reflected in manila file folders, handwritten notes, court transcripts, sentencing and probation reports, police reports, witness depositions, and Post-its with cryptic messages to myself. When I had the basics in my head, I called some of the names that repeated themselves—girlfriends, victims, arresting officers. Many didn't want to talk with me. Harry's disappearance had been like the flushing of a toilet that had been blocked for weeks, and people wanted the waste to flow away and never be brought up again.

One who did return my message was Ben Wayne Johnson. He expressed sympathy with my need to know as much as I could about the man who had wanted to kill me, and through him I found out more about Harry's scam against the old ladies. Harry had faked finding long-lost relatives and talked women into spending their meager savings on bringing those relatives to the states. That con had been his most successful and I was relieved that I had never represented him on charges relating to it. He called the play "The Lonely Widow" and he had run it about a year before he had hooked me up with the Santos family. He had not been arrested for that action but he had revealed it to me in the course of discussing another charge that had been brought against him. He had quit the Lonely Widow, he assured me, and the attorney-client privilege had kept my mouth shut about what he had confided to me.

My notes in the file indicated that I had pried loose some names from Harry and for my own well-being I had done some checking and confirmed the identities of two of Harry's victims. One had reported her case to the police, but she had died before the cops were able to pull together a solid case. The other victim, Filomena Delarosa, had not responded to my phone calls and eventually I got a message that the number had been disconnected. I had not thought through what I would have done if I had found Mrs. Delarosa, but I wanted to believe that I would have wrung some type of restitution from Harry for her. When I couldn't track her down, I had told myself that I had at least tried. The sacred attorney-client privilege had not been violated. It was slim consolation but it was all I had at the time.

Officer Johnson was very helpful. He knew where Mrs. Delarosa lived, knew quite a bit about her, in fact.

"Her sons and daughters decided that she was too frail to be on her own. They played around with putting her in a nursing home, but no one had the heart. She lives with one of her daughters, Francine Gallegos, up in Globeville, not too far from that theater group's building. You know, the old Elyria School?"

"El Centro Su Teatro? That the group you mean?"

"Yeah. Those uppity Chicano actors. Gallegos has a house on Vine. The old lady stays there. Doesn't ever leave, from what I hear. After your pal López got what he could out of her, she lost her house. The family moved her around for a while until she finally ended up with Gallegos."

"And she lives there now?"

"As far as I know. I didn't have to keep tabs on her when it turned out there wasn't a case being built by the DA's office on Harry's Lonely Widow scam."

"Delarosa's testimony wasn't enough?"

"She never wanted to testify and her family protected her. They worried that she couldn't take it—the court proceedings and all that baloney you defense attorneys pull. I only found out about her from the first lady who filed a complaint. She had been a friend of Mrs. Delarosa's. Had turned Harry on to her. So she gave us her name. But then that first woman, Baca, I think, died. And that was it."

"Thanks, Ben. I owe you one."

"You got that right."

Globeville was the kind of place that reminded everyone what it meant to be a survivor in this country. The neighborhood had always been neglected until a dog food plant or a new exit off the Interstate needed to be built. But the people were a tightly-knit community of large families that keep on in the face of low-paying or non-existent jobs, toxic contamination, and noise and diesel smoke from trucks that used the streets as shortcuts. The place carried the ambience of mid-twentieth century industrial congestion and new millennium racial shunning—the thinking was that if those people were ignored long enough maybe they would go away.

From where I stood, on her small but neat wooden porch, Filomena Delarosa didn't look like she was going anywhere.

She was a small, wrinkled woman, only slightly taller than Michael's daughter Donna and probably weighing half as much. She squinted at me from eyes almost submerged in dark chocolate folds of worn skin. She wore a gray dress, black shoes, and black stockings and the only protection against the cool fall air was a black shawl draped across her shoulders.

"*¿Qué quieres? ¿Por qué me molestas? ¿Quién eres?*"

I did what I could to communicate with her in Spanish. She was a forceful person and at first insisted that she didn't need an *abogado*. "*No tengo problemas con la policía,*" she informed me. It took several minutes but finally she seemed to acknowledge that I wanted only to talk to her about her unfortunate mix-up with Harry López.

She never invited me in her house so we talked on the porch. There, in the cold and windy evening, the tiny, animated woman screamed her words at me, because she had difficulty hearing, I assumed, and I raised my voice hoping that volume made up for the mistakes in my Spanish. We shouted at each other for fifteen minutes before we both gave up. She retreated back into her house. She insisted that I was asking for money for Harry López, something she angrily refused to do.

But I couldn't shake the feeling that she knew exactly what I was talking about all along. She understood English, and probably spoke it better than I, of that I was sure of simply because, despite what she said, the woman appeared to make sense of my wild mix of Spanish, English and legalese.

Her last comment cinched my assumption that Mrs. Delarosa was more aware of things than she would ever let on to me.

"*¿Por qué quieres dinero para López? ¡Canalla!* May he burn in hell forever."

She shut the door in my face leaving me to ponder whether she was expressing a heartfelt wish, or divulging that she knew about López's death even though the cops had kept it out of the news.

She was withered and aged but I had recognized something about the way her face tilted at me, a haughtiness that touched a nerve, a gleam in her brown slits of eyes that looked too deep into my own eyes. For several minutes I sat behind the steering wheel of my car, using my rear view mirror to stare at nothing through my replacement rear window. Emilio or Harry had put a bullet through the original glass the night an unknown, gun-toting delivery man had saved my hide. The shooter must have been Harry, I concluded, since Emilio had other targets in mind that night and he only used me for cover, for a diversion. Harry had finally trusted him and that was when Emilio shot a bullet through his head, springing on Harry the final, deadly surprise.

I would never forget Harry's look as he died, but even more clear in my memory was Emilio's face as he finished his ugly business with cold, professional expertise. Emilio's haughty face, Emilio's deep eyes . . .

Filomena Delarosa, the woman I had been shouting at on her front porch, had to be the grandmother or great-grandmother of the only Mexican hit man I had ever met.

I rested my head on the steering wheel.

"*¡Qué chingada!*"

NINETEEN

"HOW STUPID AM I?" It was a rhetorical question but Assistant District Attorney Rolanda Alvarez had an answer for me.

"If you shot yourself in the head, there wouldn't be enough brain splatter to mess the wall."

She had wrung a conviction from her jury in the murder trial and now was feeling so good about herself that she preened and pranced like a male peacock, a comparison she would have appreciated if I had had the nerve to make it.

"Is that a suggestion?"

"Take it anyway you want it. And actually, it's not that you don't have the brains, you just don't use them."

The fact that the ex sister-in-law resented that I hadn't "made more" of myself was old news and I didn't want to go there. I cut her off with some admissions that I hoped would catch her by surprise so we could get on with my need to enlist her help.

"I know it, Rolanda. I lost my cool with Boudin, when I should have gone along with him, found out what the hell he was up to. At the time I wasn't in the mood for conversation. But he obviously had something in mind when he tried to steer me against my nephew. And I didn't find out what that was."

"Yeah, that's one."

I bit the inside of my cheek and swallowed blood. Her resemblance to my ex-wife came from the way she treated me, not anything physical. The effect on me was the same, whether from Gloria, wife number one, or Rolanda, sister-in-law number one.

"And two would be, uh . . . . Maybe you can help me with that one."

"Louie, you should have called me or the police when this guy Emilio contacted you and you knew he had snatched your girlfriend. The police are trained to deal with those situations. They could have nabbed him and maybe kept that scumbag López alive."

"Or maybe not. The police have been known to make situations worse, or haven't you noticed the rash of shootings by cops that turn out to be mistakes, or unprovoked, or overreactions?"

Her anger was visible and I was losing whatever opportunity I had for her help.

"Look," I said, "I know what you mean, really. I screwed up. I'm admitting that. But now I'm ready to do it your way, the right way, with your help and with the police."

She let out a big breath of air. She could be quite patronizing when she thought it helped her make a point.

"All right, all right. But I'm a little lost, Louie. Exactly what is it that you need help with? Boudin's gone. Even my friend in the Justice Department can't tell me anything about him. He's AWOL, or whatever they call it with those undercover guys. That's what I had wanted to tell you. The DEA considers him a rogue agent, a 'walking time bomb,' as he was described to me."

"No surprise there. He should have been taken off the streets years ago."

She agreed with a nod of her head and added, "And López is dead. You know who killed *him*. It sounds like the shooter isn't after you. What else is there?"

"Two people who hired me were killed, Rolanda. I'm still working for them. That fact keeps flapping in the wind and slapping me in the face."

"But there's a major investigation going on about those deaths. A grand jury's in session! What can you do that the top law enforcement agencies of this state can't do? Give it a rest, Louie! Take a vacation."

"Take a vacation" had become the standard advice for Louie Móntez. Everyone from my secretary to my nephew to the ex sister-in-law had suggested it for me. But I was not in the mood for a beach or a casino or Disneyland. I was on my own excursion through Fantasyland, and the ride was not anywhere near close to over.

"I promise. Soon as I get a few more answers I'm out of here. Cancún, or Los Cabos. Always liked it down there. I'll get out of your hair and everyone can relax. Promise."

I held up my hand, mimicking making an oath on my grandmother's bible and gave her what I hoped was my most sincere look—half of a smile, eye-to-eye contact, and not a trace of sarcasm.

Another deep sigh. "Okay. What do you want?"

"Great, Rolanda. I really appreciate it. I . . ."

"Yeah, yeah. Just get on with it."

"Right. This thing started with me being asked to help Dominic Santos. Well, we all know he had a very bad accident before I got into the case. But I think I need to go back to square one, back to Dominic. I know something about him from his father and his, uh, wife. From the newspaper articles, and even a bit from Tyler Boudin. If I could get the rest of it, maybe something will fall in place."

She squirmed in her seat behind her cluttered desk. "Like what, Louie? Be specific."

"His file from his stretch in the New Mexico pen, for one. That's where he met this guy Boudin. Maybe there's something there. Or any police reports or incident write-ups from other police jurisdictions, like the local Alamosa police or the CBI. Anything like that. Even stuff about the remaining members of the family, the estranged brother and sister. That kind of information. It will probably amount to nothing, but maybe it will get me off this kick and I can take that vacation. It should be worth it to you just to see me leave town, no?"

Yet another deep sigh. "This is it, Louie. You're way over your share of favors from me. Gloria hates your guts, you know. Your boys still like you, though, and they are my nephews. So, that's something. But this is it. I mean it."

"Great, Rolanda. I mean it, too. No more begging for favors. Like I said, I promise."

I had a similar conversation with Ben Wayne Johnson, without the lectures, and I asked him for any additional information on the family of Filomena Delarosa. He agreed to forward what he could dig up since he had taken a special interest in Harry López's victims and that group included not only Filomena but Louie Móntez, too.

Maybe I expected too much from the two law enforcement types. Maybe I should have looked back at all the times district attorneys and cops had played with the lives of my clients like they were arranging paper dolls in toy houses, discarding the ones slightly torn, worn out, or not pretty enough to prop up for display. Maybe I should have remembered lessons I had learned in my youth about not trusting The Man, about realizing what side I really was on. But to do that I would have had to ignore that Ben Wayne Johnson and Rolanda Alvarez were supposed to try to do the right thing if for no other reason than the almost matching shades of our respective skin colors. That had to be enough because if the two law enforcement types couldn't unearth just a kernel of the buried truth, then where did that leave me?

From my chair I could look through an office window out across the not yet trendy Golden Triangle landscape. I thought, another year or two and the office rent will be out of my sole practitioner budget. Another five years and the building will be converted to condos, if it remains at all.

The sun was a frosted glass marble mostly hidden by gray and dirty white clouds that kept the city cold and on the verge of a storm. An unexpected chill caused me to shudder and I put on my suit coat and walked around my office.

I didn't take a drink from the desk bottle, again. I didn't call Alicia, again.

What I did was immerse myself in all the information I could get on the water war in the valley. I had newspaper clippings, the files that Fermín Santos had made available to me, and some more case work from Max Macías. I made a few phone calls. The time slipped away like the last dead leaves of autumn.

The case had turned into a monster for the plaintiffs. Max and his legal team had to overcome outdated theories, dead or aging witnesses, and years of custom and practice that a federal court had qualms about ignoring. In the end, they had failed and the loss had been a blow to the valley people and the lawyers who had invested their reputations on the case. But everyone who commented on the outcome had concluded that the fight had been a good fight—a worthy but hopeless cause.

Eventually, after my eyes burned from too much reading and my brain ached from what I had learned, I left the loneliness of my office and approached Rosa at her desk. It had taken hours but when I started to see the answer it became as obvious as Alicia's advice that I needed to cut back on my drinking. Rosa finished a phone call then looked up at me.

"I'm going to visit Max Macías. He's home now, too sick to go in to his office. One of his daughters told me it was okay to go by his house. I guess I should pay my respects."

Her mouth turned upward, but it wasn't a smile. She said, "You're taking it hard. Why so serious? Does he affect you that much?"

"It is a sad thing, Rosa. In many ways. The man was a pioneer around here. He started organizations and projects that go on to this day. Scholarships for kids from the projects. One of the founders of what later turned into the Hispanic Bar Association. So many important cases for so many people. He should have been the first Mexican justice on the state supreme court."

"And that's why you look like your best friend died? Because Max Macías is leaving us and it will be a great loss?"

I grabbed my topcoat from the coat rack near Rosa's desk, wrapped a scarf around my neck, and made sure I had my car keys.

"Isn't that enough?"

It wasn't enough, of course. But Rosa wouldn't have known that. I think at that time, on that day when I couldn't warm up, when the earth shivered in expectation of an icy blast from the Northwest, I was one of only two people who knew that the tragedy of Max Macías had very little to do with his rapidly approaching death. Max was the other one.

When Rosa asked me about my apparent depression over visiting Max, I hinted at the emotion I felt because one of my teachers and role models was facing his last illness. I didn't tell her that I had to confront the dying man on either his incompetence or his corruption. I wouldn't have been able to explain it to her. I couldn't explain it to myself.

TWENTY

I WAITED IN my car outside of Max's large, handsome house for several minutes. I wasn't sure I was ready for my visit with the older attorney. He lived in a fashionable Tudor style home on Tennyson immediately north of I-70, a small neighborhood of persons who had enough money to live in the quiet and theoretically safer confines of the suburbs, but who had chosen instead to live on the edge of the city, close to the Willis Case golf course, Berkeley Lake Park, Federal Boulevard *taquerías*, and the buzz of Denver proper. The house represented new money but good taste. Nothing ostentatious, simply well done.

A silver metallic Mercedes-Benz SUV sat in the street in front of Max's house. The vanity plates read "MB".

I watched a man leave Max's house and climb into the SUV. He wore an orange hunting vest and a tan Stetson as his only protection against the cold. From a distance, he looked like Ross Perot in western gear.

Several minutes passed before the door opened in response to my persistent pressing of the doorbell. I was mildly surprised when Max himself appeared. He had always been tough, and independent. Why should he change a lifetime of attitude just to accommodate the dying process?

A smile broke out across his face but it faded as quickly as the wispy snowflakes that melted on the wool of my coat. He shuffled back in his house and I followed him. His gaudy suspenders and flashy ties had been replaced with a robe and slippers. An acrid, subtle odor followed him—the smell of chemicals, drugs, and finality.

In a raspy, thin voice, he said, "So good of you to come by, Luis. Can I offer you something?"

His eyes were sunken and his skin had turned a chalky gray. I did not want to look at him as I talked but I forced myself. He was entitled to at least that. I kept my coat on and dripped sleety ice on his soft carpet. My wet shoes left smudges of mud. He didn't notice or he didn't care.

"No thank you, Max. I'm fine, except for being a little cold."

He had a blanket draped across his back and he offered it to me. I declined.

He nodded and said, "Once the cold gets in your bones there's not much a person can do about it."

"Max, is there anything I can do for you? Anything you need?"

"That's kind, Luis. But, I have everything. A nurse, medicines, my children and wife on hand for my every whim. They're all upstairs, waiting for me to come up so they can put me back in bed. I hate it, though. I'm really appreciative of the company."

A woman's laughter and a young man's whispered response drifted down the stairs.

"Is that why Matthew Barber was here? A visit to pass the time away?"

He hesitated as he was about to sit on a lounge chair that had an extra pillow on the seat. When he was comfortable he spoke again, the voice more subdued, weaker.

"If I were a superstitious man, Luis, I might speculate on the coincidence that you, an old friend, choose to visit me on the same day as one of my oldest enemies. Somehow, it seems right. ¿No? And, I insisted that he come to me. One last visit. We know so much about each other that we are compelled to do as the other wants. A real Mexican stand-off."

He cleared his throat and continued, "Even Cora asked me about him. She doesn't understand, of course. But . . . I assume you do, don't you, Luis? A man like you, with your history, your outlook, you would understand because Barber being at my house doesn't surprise you, does it? It's almost what you would expect from a man like me, someone you once called a *vendido*."

That term again. *Vendido*. Sellout. It's what Harry López had called me only seconds before his life had ended so surprisingly and swiftly. I had used it in reference to many others: anyone who didn't quite see the world as I did, anyone who wasn't willing to make the same choices I made, anyone who wouldn't pay the price to live their lives the way I thought I was supposed to live mine. What it had meant, and what it had come to mean, were lost on me as I stood over Max. Concepts like *vendido* didn't seem to matter, anymore. But I was sure of one thing. I had never called Max Macías a sellout.

I gave him my best argument. I tried to be precise and convincing—a professional, a good lawyer, just as he had taught me for so many years.

I said, "At the beginning, there had been small things. In the early years of the case your legal team had problems meeting court-imposed deadlines. Pleadings were filed late, discovery requests were delayed or not dealt with, and motions for continuances became a standard mode of operation for the plaintiffs. The attorneys on the team had to spend valuable resources asking for extensions of time to respond to motions from the defendants, or to file legal briefs, or to take the depositions of key witnesses. These things happen, especially in a complicated federal case with numerous claims and allegations. By themselves, the incidents of professional malingering didn't amount to more than the fallout from busy attorneys stretched to their limits for a pro bono case that threatened to swamp them all."

He glared at me.

"But then I looked at the way the case was argued. I read the briefs, the various opinions along the way, and the cases that were cited on behalf of both sides. The defendants always seemed to be able to distinguish and minimize the case law that the plaintiffs presented, yet the plaintiffs never quite responded in kind. That, too, could be explained. After all, in every lawsuit, there is a winner and a loser. Who knows that better than you?"

He did not say anything.

"Often, the case opinions favor one side over the other but, just as often, the case law can be read to support both sides and the judge has to interpret that law, apply the law to the facts, and make a decision that could go either way but because there is enough to justify it, the decision will stand the scrutiny of an appeals court. Except that in this case, the plaintiffs, the people of the valley who were fighting for their water rights, were behind the eight ball throughout the litigation."

Finally, he muttered, "You've got it wrong. So wrong."

I ignored him and kept at it. "I learned that two key players in the case, elderly residents of the valley who had firsthand information about the use of the water for decades, had not been deposed early on, and that by the time the plaintiffs wanted to set up the depositions, one witness had died and the other had become infirm and unable to testify. There's not any excuse for that, Max. And several attorneys quit the case over the years, often claiming that they were burned out or needed a break or had to get on with making their own career."

"Some of them just gave up, Luis. They couldn't take it."

I had taken a chance and called one of those attorneys, now safely ensconced in his own partnership track at a downtown firm, but he had been very guarded with me and wary of why I would be calling on a case that he had deserted years before. Even so, I could read from his responses that the problem for him had been the handling of the case by the lead counsel, Max. When he first got involved with the case, he had been a young, eager, liberal lawyer, fresh out of law school. Any disillusionment he suffered would have been muted, especially in the face of the reputation of Max Macías. He had understood his role as a white man in a case run by a well-regarded Latino lawyer and brought on behalf of clients who were primarily poor Chicanos, and he would have quietly exited without raising any of his concerns. I knew the type and if I had been wrong in misinterpreting his responses to me, I wasn't too far off the mark.

My time with Max was short but as ugly as a cockfight. Eventually, he tried to explain what he thought had happened. He admitted that Barber admired him for putting up "a good fight" and that they had reached a mutual agreement that was better for everybody involved. Max attempted to convince me that Barber's visit showed respect, even if it had been made at Max's insistence. Max's voice trailed off as he talked and I didn't respond. The sounds from the people upstairs had diminished until all I heard was the creak from the floor beneath his chair as Max's spent body shifted on the pillow. Finally, he whispered, "It should have been the biggest case of my career. It turned out to be the saddest. And, now, God is punishing me, Luis. You see that, don't you?"

"I see only that you let down so many people, Max. Barber bought you off, there's no other way to say it."

He wanted an answer that might mean forgiveness, or a curse that acknowledged his guilt. I couldn't give either of those to him. Max had committed the sin that Harry López had accused me of, only Max wouldn't accept it.

"Why, Max? Why?"

He shuddered and pulled the blanket closer to his chest.

"Barber had all the cards, Luis! He had the lawyers, the experts, the money. And what did we have? A bunch of volunteer do-gooders, Mariele's and the old man's rhetoric, and that was it. No money. No experts. No damn help."

His face reddened and his breath came in gasps. His chest heaved and he began to cough. He sat in the chair for several minutes, coughing, shuddering, and not looking at me. When his body calmed down he tried to explain it to me again.

"I did the best job I could for the people who mattered. Barber needed workers on his ranch—I got men jobs. The valley needed business, investment—I got money for the valley. I could have helped even old man Santos, if only he had not been so goddamn stubborn! Barber was ready to share the water rights. He was spending hundreds of thousands of dollars on that damn lawsuit. He wanted it to end. He agreed to hire men from the valley, he set up some businesses. If only Fermín had eased up, if only his goddamn son had stayed out of it! He would have been all right. But he wouldn't do it. He just wouldn't do it. And so, he lost it all. We both did. In the end, when it was over and Barber knew I had made it easy for him to win, he wanted to give me something, too. He had come through on the jobs, on the new business, even on a scholarship fund for children of the valley. You have to know, Luis. I didn't accept a damn thing from him."

I walked away from him and out of his house without looking back.

The storm had arrived and snow fell earnestly and completely. Large flakes covered my car. I used my bare hand to sweep them from the windshield. They were thin and dry. My throat felt rough and the chill had rooted along my spine. And yet, I sweated as I started up the car and drove away. My face felt damp and clammy. I thought that I must have a fever. A bead of sweat rolled down my cheek. I wiped it away. Sweating in a snow storm. It must have been sweat.

Rosa handed me a package that had been sent to me by courier. There was no return address, no letter, no memo, no indication of who had mailed the documents but I made a note to buy Rolanda Alvarez a bouquet of flowers or a box of candy. The package included copies of records from the New Mexico Department of Corrections on Dominic Santos and Tyler Boudin, as well as statements taken from numerous witnesses for the arson that had occurred on Matthew Barber's property. The more I read, the more I admired Rolanda. Flowers or candy would not be enough, and that meant that I couldn't send her anything to thank her. I couldn't compromise her or risk that she would have to explain herself to somebody in the DEA, or to her boss, Daniel Galena.

It's all in the paperwork, I thought. Follow the paper trail, first for Max Macías, then Dominic Santos.

Santos had been mixed up in the flourishing drug trade that had its center in the San Luis Valley, of that I was sure and so, apparently, were several law enforcement agencies. Rolanda's office had prepared a memo meant for a combined state and federal task force that focused on Dominic's role as a highly paid bag man, just as Tyler Boudin had told me. Santos had used his prison connections to barge in on the profitable business, and

Boudin had tagged along for the ride. Santos had been kept on ice in the Denver jail to buy the task force time to get its ducks lined up. Boudin had been sent in to the jail to keep an eye on his old *compadre* from the New Mexico pen. The arson had been a very convenient handle to grab Santos, but his death in the jail riot had been most inconvenient for the task force and its million dollar operation. Without him, Boudin had nothing to corroborate his work. Boudin's entry into the drug business died with Dominic Santos. After years of undercover work, the death of his snitch might have been enough to push Boudin over the thin edge that he had straddled for much too long. But was it enough to explain the wild accusation he had made against Michael Torres?

"It sounds like he cracked up and just said the first thing that hatched in his head."

Rosa was very sure of herself. She had listened to my review of what I had learned from Rolanda's delivery and answered my question with her usual self-confidence. She had a good head on her shoulders, although that head often carried multi-hued hair, pieces of metal stuck in the strangest places, leather and steel dog collars, and other accoutrements of a youthful style that I would never adopt for my own, no matter how trendy it became. She didn't need the recently-acquired chrome pin protruding through her eyebrow. I would have given good odds that somewhere under the strange and colorful outfits a red rose tattoo rested, embedded in Rosa's skin. As far as I knew, her appearance hadn't cost me any walk-in business. But then, how would I know?

She rushed her words, not bothering to breathe while she spoke.

"Boudin had planned to bust this big criminal operation but he needed the help of Dominic Santos, who was involved in that operation and who Boudin knew from prior *cochinadas* that they both had been mixed up in. Santos gets busted for the fire, and Boudin goes to jail, too, to keep an eye on his man, and probably to turn him completely. But, Santos, who also has a wild reputation, gets himself killed in a jailhouse riot, sending the already crazy Boudin into limbo land."

I took a breath for her and added, "I think that's the way it played out, Rosa. Boudin starts to scramble and he comes to me, probably hoping that whatever contact I had with the Santos family led me to something, or someone, he could tap for his case."

She winked at me, a habit I did not like or encourage but one that didn't seem likely to pass away soon. "When you go crazy yourself, he says something to throw you off, and I guess it worked, although you trip out even more. Then he disappears back under the rock he crawled from. You think he killed Mr. Santos and Mariele?"

I paused, thought about my answer to her question.

"Yeah, I guess I do. He fits just because he was around, and because he's a lunatic. But why? There's no reason for those two to be killed. Not any that I can come up with, anyway."

She opened a pack of gum and offered me a stick, which I declined. Between chews she said, "You told me once that sometimes the best defenses for your clients were the most obvious, the simplest, because the jury understood them and they often made the most sense. Like: Our guy did the stabbing but he was forced into it by the other guy. Our client didn't break into the house but he bought stolen goods from the person who probably did do the burglary. The eyewitness is sure of his ID but everyone knows eyewitness testimony has inherent flaws. You just have to dig out those flaws in the particular case. You've told me all that. Doesn't that work here?"

"Something obvious about the deaths of Fermín Santos and Mariele Castilla? God, what could that be?"

She noisily chewed her gum and I thought about Mariele. A troubled lady, with scars to prove it. Did she kill herself and the old man? Again, why? They had been found naked, in bed. Were they lovers? Was that too much to believe, even about Mariele?

Rosa said, "They offended somebody, unless it was a murder-suicide. Who could those two upset that much? Barber? Boudin? Michael? Emilio? Who's left?"

She surprised me with her list. Was my nephew now a suspect in the murders of Santos and Castilla, just after we had cleared him of making threats against Alicia?

I asked, "Did Alicia have a motive?"

"Please, Luis, that doesn't even deserve to be said. Unless you think she could get stupid jealous over you, since that's the only connection, right? No, no. Don't even go there. It's crazy. It's all crazy. Boudin's your man. Watch your back, Luis." She left my office and returned to answering the phones and dealing with the business of my practice.

She was right. I could eliminate Alicia from the list that I regretted had ever been compiled. Her and Max Macías and Harry López and Dominic Santos could all rest easily, some in their graves. They were either dead or too sick or too close to me to be considered suspects in the murders of Fermín Santos and Mariele Castilla. Tyler Boudin, he was the one. The motive would have to be revealed later. That's the way it was supposed to work.

TWENTY-ONE

BEN WAYNE JOHNSON stood at the front door of my house dressed in civilian clothes. For him that meant jeans, a down vest, a plaid flannel shirt with shiny snaps. He could have just climbed off the bus from Window Rock. The guy next to him definitely was not from the reservation. His hair was cropped short, and his shiny black skin bounced the glare of my porch light. A gray Chesterfield and gray leather gloves protected him from the cold that apparently didn't bother Johnson. I nodded at the two cops and they entered my house.

Johnson got right to it.

"Louie, this is John Reed. He's with the DEA. He wants to talk with you about your different encounters with Boudin, and what you know about the Santos killings. He thought if he came with me, you'd be more open to him. I didn't promise him anything, Louie. But, it may be in your interest to at least hear him out."

Reed removed his right glove and offered his hand in greeting. I shook it and motioned that they should sit down. Reed took off his coat but Johnson sat down without changing anything. The DEA man wore a dark gray suit and rimless glasses, and clenched his teeth a lot. He was one of those men that other men respect almost immediately. He looked strong.

Reed said, "My interest is in bringing down Al Morales.

He's gone bad. We need to stop him before he endangers any civilians, or agency operations. I think you can help me."

I knew immediately the implications of what he had said. Habit required me to ask the question anyway.

"Who's Al Morales?"

"Alberto Trinidad Morales. DEA undercover agent. You know him as Tyler Boudin."

"Boudin's a Mexican?!"

Reed looked quizzically at Johnson, who shrugged.

"Well, he's certainly some kind of Hispanic. Born in the States, his mother was from Texas, maiden name Cisneros. She died before Morales was a year old. Morales's file doesn't have anything on the father, other than a name, Leonardo Caspar Morales. Morales was raised in a San Antonio orphanage. Brilliant guy, scholarship student at UT, Navy SEAL, then worked his way up quickly in the agency, but he got bogged down on his last assignment, the San Luis Valley drug cartel. Like I said, he's gone bad, and we need to bring him in."

The winter moon poured yellow light through my front window, exposing us to anyone who walked by. I pulled on the drape cords for privacy but caught a brief glimpse of the outside. A coat of white rested on the ground and trees, the fence and Johnson's car. The snow vibrated in the moonlight and a thousand phony diamonds sparkled across my yard. Patches of dark, frozen mud broke the snow and ice cover in the struggle between the weather and the earth. It matched my own struggle to understand a man like Tyler Boudin. Alberto Morales would always be Tyler Boudin to me.

"And you want me to help you?"

Reed slowly rubbed his hands together as though they were still cold.

"I just want to go over everything that happened between the two of you. He's disappeared, vanished from the screen, so anything you know might help. What did he want with you, what did he say, how did he act? You may not realize what you really know until someone else hears it, right?"

I didn't mind playing his detective game. His ability to generate respect only went so far, of course, but I also thought that if I went through it all again something might click in my own head. I had Boudin targeted as the killer of Fermín Santos and Mariele Castilla and, maybe, John Reed could help confirm that for me.

I gave Reed all I had, my suspicions, the nastiness from my brief conversations with the rogue agent, the details of our fights. He took copious notes, made few remarks, and kept his opinions about my behavior to himself.

Ben Wayne Johnson added what he knew, which wasn't much about Boudin, but during that long talk that night he did bring up that he had done some checking for me and, although he thought it wouldn't add to what we knew about Boudin, Reed wanted to hear that, too. Johnson had learned that Filomena Delarosa had several grandchildren, many of whom were respectable members of the community. One, however, had disappeared a few years ago when he ran from the law because of an armed robbery caper gone bad. That grandson's name was Emiliano Zapata Madero, but he was called "EZ" or Emilio. Emilio Madero had several outstanding warrants but he had slipped away as thoroughly as Boudin.

Reed said, "These aren't the same guy, are they? Both men follow you, accost you, pull guns on you, threaten you, and then pull a Houdini. You attract some odd attention, Móntez."

"Including from the DEA."

He pursed his lips and nodded.

"Including from the DEA, the Denver PD, the CBI, a state grand jury, even *Sixty Minutes*. You're a sought-after kind of guy."

"Never heard from *Sixty Minutes*. Didn't need that."

"Would have helped your practice, don't you think? Going *mano a mano* with Ed Bradley on national TV certainly would have stirred up some business. Look what the limelight did for Johnny Cochrane."

"Yeah. Right."

I didn't ask him any questions because I assumed that he wouldn't answer me unless it helped his cause, and I couldn't count on him telling me the truth, anyway. I liked the guy, and was willing to help him, but I also couldn't shake the feeling that I was dealing with a man who knew exactly how to get what he wanted, and how not to give up anything. John Reed lived in control mode.

At the end of the conversation Reed admitted that he didn't know where to go next. His job was to find Tyler Boudin and bring him in. He wasn't working on the San Luis Valley water war or the murders of Santos or Castilla or even the drug business that had sprouted in the valley. He had one objective—Boudin, but he didn't have a plan. I gave him one.

"Boudin tried to talk with me. He thought I might know something that could make up for losing Dominic Santos. He lied to me about my nephew to get me to back off. Ben and his partner arrived and he couldn't finish whatever it was he had started with me. Then he walked away from the hospital using his DEA credentials and he hasn't tried to contact me since. But, I think that's because he changed his mind about me. He decided I wasn't of any use. I didn't know anything that could help him. But, what if he thinks that I now *do* know something that will help him? Or hurt him? Maybe that I'm going to reveal something about him that will end whatever it is that he thinks he's got left with the agency, or with the drug honchos? What if he thinks he has to contact me?"

Reed cleared his throat. He said, "You're talking about making yourself bait. A trap for a man that understands all about sting operations, set-ups and double-crosses. It ain't gonna happen. Number one, we can't risk it. If you, a civilian, get hurt, killed more likely, the agency suffers in all kinds of ways, not the least of which is too much scrutiny from the press and a Congressional oversight committee. Number two, there's nothing that would bring out Boudin. He's on the run, from us and from whomever he thought he was going to bust with Dominic's help. It won't work. I admire your, uh, ambition. But, we won't have anything to do with that kind of plan."

I leaned back in my couch. The house had become comfortable for me over the years. I had managed to discard all the remnants of previous wives, roommates, and significant others. The place had my music, my books, my trash piled up in the corners. John Reed did not fit in with my house. He was too neat, too much in control, and way on the other side of the criminal justice system fence. In my house, he had to listen.

"You don't have to be officially involved. If it goes haywire, you can step back and blame it on me. You tried to stop me, you didn't know what I was up to. Whatever. All you *have* to do is let the right people know that I have come up with something that proves Tyler Boudin killed Mariele Castilla and Fermín Santos. The right people are those people in the agency and on the streets who will make sure that Boudin's ears prick up to the news. I'm going to spread the same kind of message to people I know who just might have a way of passing on a message to Boudin, or someone who knows Boudin. Guys like some of my former clients, guys in the joint who owe me a favor, punks like Harry López, even a few cops who know how to get messages delivered. Then, I'm going back to the valley. The word will be that I'm going to confirm what I think I know. He will believe something really is coming down if I go back there. In fact, you could get me a pass to old man Santos's house. No one bothers me from the Alamosa cops or the DEA, if you say so. Tomorrow night. No time for Boudin to think this through. I'll be there. With any luck, Tyler Boudin will be, too. He and I have never gotten along, so our meeting will probably end up like the others—one of us bleeding on the ground. If you are around, you can get in on the party. If you're not, it could end badly."

Reed stood up and slipped on his nice coat.

"Why would you do this? What can you get out of this, except more grief, maybe death? What's it to you, Móntez?"

I looked up at the man who seemed to be in control of his universe, and who looked completely out of place in mine.

"It's a lot of things. The way he tried to implicate my nephew, and use a friend of mine. His negative involvement with an important piece of Chicano history. The beating he gave me. A retainer I still have to earn."

I stopped and Reed nodded. He said, "But that's not all of it."

His eyes told me he understood. I said, "It's Boudin's self-hate thing. That bothers me, bothers me almost too much. That guy hated me simply because of my background, a background we shared. I've got to ask him about that. Maybe we can talk about it. Maybe we won't talk at all. That's all I can say, Reed. All the explanation I got."

Ben Wayne Johnson opened my front door. He said, "You're crazy, man, but *buena suerte, amigo*."

He walked out the door and into the cold night. Reed looked at me and touched his forehead with two fingers. It was a way of saying goodbye but it looked like a salute. I liked that. As I said, Reed had a way of getting what he wanted.

The rest of that night consisted of a flurry of phone calls and quick trips to pool halls, bars, and the house parties that seem to go on permanently for some people, like my clients. I stopped by the Billiards Centre and made sure several of the players heard me talking about my planned trip. On a bulletin board near the front counter was a bad copy of a photograph of Harry López with the caption "Missing—Reward for Information." Harry had a few friends who cared enough to scrape together $1000 for a lead. That money would never be collected. For a second I played around with the idea that maybe I could make a claim to the reward for my unpaid fees.

I called anyone I could think of who might drop the word that I was onto something big and dangerous and that I was going down to the valley to end it, once and for all. I woke up several people, many of whom didn't take kindly to my interruption of their Thursday night. Michael Torres tried to talk me out of my scheme. Deputy Sheriff Danny Frésquez thought I was crazy. Rolanda Alvarez didn't return my voice mail message. Max's wife, Cora, answered the phone and took my message but I don't think she understood and I doubted that she passed it on to Max. I called Alicia again and there was no answer and no answering machine. Finally, around midnight, I called my father in Fort Collins.

"Goddam, Louie. Who died? You know what time it is? This better be important. I could have had a heart attack. You can't call an old man at this time of night. You woke up everybody in the house. What's the problem, *hijo?*"

"Just called to say hello, Dad. Haven't been around much, lately, and I didn't want you to forget about your favorite son."

"Are you drunk? This ain't funny, Louie."

He shouted a string of Mexican epithets that slandered my ancestry, which was his, too, of course. When he finished, he said, "So, what's the problem? You got something to tell me, now's the chance."

"No, really, Dad. It's just been a while since we talked. You know I love these father/son talks of ours. I missed them. That's all. And, I'll be coming up on Sunday. Spend some time with you. Maybe we can go out to dinner. You know? Or will you be in church all day?"

The old man thought over my words.

"Well, I'll be at services in the morning. But, there is this new Vietnamese place that I want to try out. We could go there for lunch, or dinner. Depends on how long you'll be here. So, don't worry about me and church. I'll be ready when you are."

"Great. I'll see you then."

"Louie. You sure everything's all right?"

"Dad. Don't worry so much. Can't a guy take his father to dinner? It's cool."

He smirked. "*Sí. Un poquito frío*. Downright freezing. Okay, *hijo*. See you on Sunday."

TWENTY-TWO

MY DRIVE TO the valley was very different from the ride I had taken when I thought I was on a trip to talk an old man out of a wild idea. I started early, around six a.m. The city was in darkness but the traffic had geared up for another rush hour. I drove slowly, cautiously, and without anger. I endured the antics of other drivers and didn't take their stupid mistakes as personal affronts. I had a calmness that surprised me, and I went with it.

But when I drove through Pueblo the calm deserted me. I exited at the turn-off to Alicia's house, and then I reentered the freeway as soon as I could. I executed a U-turn in the middle of an intersection because my mind was racing faster than my car's engine. Traffic near me braked and honked, and a burly Chicano in a knit cap glared at me as I zigged and zagged my way around him to the freeway entrance. I thought I had wanted to stop and see Alicia, talk with her, let her know what I was doing, but then I remembered that she had caught a bus out of Denver and never looked back. I traveled south, relentlessly, quietly, and without more sidetracks from my objective.

In Alamosa, I didn't bother to check in at a motel. I parked my car on Main Street and found a diner where I had a late, heavy breakfast. Then I walked the streets of the town, as I had on my previous visit. The San Luis Valley tourist bureau used the buzz words "cool sunshine." Sometimes that motto was true. But what I felt as I walked the long and almost deserted street was nowhere near cool. The air was frigid and penetrating. The sun perched brightly in the sky, oblivious to the wintry earth, not offering any warmth. My face numbed up, my hands started to ache, and my feet turned into clumps of cold. Finally, unable to withstand the temperature, and not seeing any immediate alternatives, I walked into a bar looking for heat.

The place was busy with young men drinking beer and playing lethargic games of pool. They ignored me. I scanned the groups of out-of-work men for Michael but he wasn't in the place.

The booths were empty and I found a seat and ordered a beer. The chubby waitress delivered it to my table and walked away with three dollars, which included a dollar tip. It was my first drink in several days. I was full from the diner breakfast but when I took a swig of the beer it flowed like warm honey. My brain perked up, my body relaxed, and my eyes saw clearly. I experienced the ruse of alcohol that I had taken for granted for many years and so had forgotten how enticing its effects could be.

I almost convinced myself that I could play some pool to pass the time, that I might even call Michael and have him meet me. The pool-playing men appeared friendly enough and the waitress needed something to do.

I realized what I was doing. That first drink had been slow and good and perfect. I didn't want to spoil it.

I carefully placed the beer on the table and grabbed my coat from the hook on the side of the booth. I walked out of the bar and returned to my car.

I spent the rest of the day with Michael and his family. I drank too much coffee, watched too many cartoons with Michael's daughters, and worked myself into a nervous bag of mindless energy.

Our evening meal consisted of refried beans, fried potatoes with onion and green pepper, and a venison stew that Michael called "deer meat menudo." I ate what I could force down my throat but I was too wound up to enjoy the food.

Over coffee, my nephew told me everything that was wrong with my plan. Michael hammered at me to leave and go back to Denver. When he accepted that I was not going to listen to him, he settled back and heard me out.

Finally, he said, "I give up. It's your funeral, *tío*. Tell me what you want me to do."

"You've got to be my lookout. But Boudin has to believe that I am alone. I get to the house alone. You come up the back way—there must be a path or road to the Santos ranch that a guy like you knows about, and not too many other people." He nodded. "Boudin will watch for a while, maybe all night. But, he *will* make his move. Then, you and I make ours."

⁙

Around ten that night, I drove to the deserted ranch house of Fermín Santos.

The ranch seemed to be further out than I remembered and Santos Ranch Road rougher and more deserted. The house was isolated, away from the highway and traffic. I drove under the Holy Earth sign and parked as close to the house as I could. I walked up the wood chip path and to the front door. Paquito, the old man's dog, did not rush me as an intruder. His time in the house, like his master's, was over.

I pushed the door and it opened for me. John Reed had taken care of the details, and it reassured me that he and other DEA agents must be watching me, hoping that Boudin would appear, while I hoped that he would give up without much of a fight.

Later, I would have to admit that I was afraid as I walked in the house. There had to be fear roiling in my guts, there must have been dread and wariness crawling all over my skin. But right then, right when the moon slipped behind the clouds and the silence overwhelmed the night, right at the instant when I stepped into the darkness of Fermín's house, I did not hesitate, I did not think about what I was doing or what might happen.

The place smelled like the old man. The years he had spent in the house had ingrained his spirit in the floors, walls, furniture. He was everywhere.

The house almost was as cold as outside. The lights didn't work. I walked slowly through the house, using a flashlight I had carried from my car. I saw clothes hanging in a closet—

heavy shirts, jean jackets, hooded parkas—dishes piled on a kitchen counter, a few boxes of knick-knacks, photograph albums, mementos of the old man's life. Someone had begun to pack things for a move to storage, or, perhaps, a second-hand store, and I assumed that the remaining members of the Santos family had returned to the house and their duties as survivors. Why weren't they in the house? Maybe they were in town, staying at a motel, ordered away by John Reed with the promise that the federal agents were closing in on the killer. Maybe they didn't want to pay for utilities that they didn't need. They could do whatever it was that needed to be done during the day. Or, maybe they simply chose not to stay in the house where their father had been murdered.

I sat on the same leather couch where I had talked with Fermín Santos on a night that clung in my memory like a part of my brain. That night, the old man had run me off because I had dared to suspect that he had hired a man to exact revenge for his son's death, and Emilio and Harry López had chased me along the deserted country road until I assumed I had escaped them and I had crawled in the back seat of my car to sleep. That night, the old man and the wife had died.

Mariele Castilla had led me to believe that the old man had hired Emilio to exact his own revenge. Fermín had set me straight on that account. She hadn't anticipated that I would visit the old man on my own. She had wanted me in the valley for her own reasons. She had wanted me to confront Emilio. In the old man's house, I guessed that she had been helping Harry. The two of them had hatched a screwball scheme that targeted me, but they had been the victims. Earlier I had been sure that Boudin had killed Mariele, but among the remnants of Fermín's life, I had my doubts. It could just as easily have been Emilio.

I waited for Tyler Boudin to burst through the door of the house. I hoped that John Reed and his men were close, ready to pounce on Boudin when he appeared. I hoped that Michael Torres had kept his word and was nearby also, ready to help me if Reed wasn't around or if Boudin got the upper hand.

But the countryside around the house had looked bleak and

empty. Reed could have set me up. He might have had no intention of saving me from Boudin. I knew too much about Boudin and his illegal ways. I could be an embarrassment to the agency. If Boudin finished me off, and the DEA covered it up, who would ever know? Who would ever care? I easily convinced myself that those types of conspiracies happened, especially to someone as expendable as me, especially if the threatened agency was as powerful and secretive as the DEA.

I walked around the house again. I couldn't warm up. I waited. The cold encased my body, slowed my blood and my heart. I caught myself drifting away several times. My body twitched periodically, and I jerked my head several times at sounds and shadows. I slipped into a state midway between sleep and consciousness.

!!i

I coughed and woke myself up. I breathed in smoke. The Santos ranch house was on fire. The front door was blocked with flames from the porch. My legs were numb and heavy. I forced myself to run through the old man's kitchen. The heat from the flames nipped at my back. I heard a crash behind me, then a wave of smoke and heat rolled over me as I ran. Panic settled in at the base of my brain. I thought of the fires from the summer when hundreds of thousands of acres of trees, brush, and wild grasses ignited and vanished in a blur of speed and ferocity. I knew the San Luis Valley was dry and still parched, suffering from the drought, even in winter, even with an early snow storm. I could be engulfed by flames, surrounded by the fire that would burn out of control, quickly and deadly.

I jerked the door open, kicked the screen out of my way and plunged into the cold night air. I kept running, eager for distance between me and the burning house. I looked over my shoulder, heard an electric, vibrant snap, and saw the house explode in a fiery, orange ball. I fell to the ground. Wood, stone, chunks of adobe fell around me. Something fell on my back and knocked the air out of my lungs. I rolled, tried to regain my breath.

Tyler Boudin stood over me, holding a rifle. He swung the rifle at my head.

✝

TWENTY-THREE

I CAME TO in the front seat of a minivan driven by Boudin. Blood trickled from my scalp down the side of my face and neck. I was dizzy and sick to my stomach. I tried to get my bearings. Only a few minutes must have passed since Boudin had pounded me into unconsciousness. We were on the back edge of the Santos Ranch, on a road that could take us either back to Alamosa or into the Great Sand Dunes National Monument.

Boudin drove in silence. He looked wild and out of control.

The sun was due to rise over the eastern end of the valley.

I groaned, then sputtered, "Where are you going? You can't get away. The feds . . ."

He slammed his fist on the dash.

"They won't do you any good, Móntez! Your buddy Reed and that meddling nephew of yours? They'll be lucky to get to you before the coyotes and buzzards pick your sorry bones clean. They were so keen on setting a trap! Dumb fucks!"

He laughed. He looked at me.

"I warned you, Móntez. More than once! I said, stay out of this! You were in way over your head. They were all dead, for chrissakes! But you came back. Begging for it! I ain't got no choice now. It's too late, now. Too late for all of us."

He screamed and cursed and swore at me as he drove along the southern boundary of the park. He incoherently lashed out at John Reed and the DEA, Mariele and Fermín, Alicia. Spit and sweat rained from his mouth and face.

"The fire at the ranch." I half-groaned, half-mumbled. "You must have had it set before I showed up. A timer, or electric fuse, to give you time to distract Reed and my nephew."

"For a dumb Mexican, sometimes you surprise me, Móntez. But you ain't no dumber than that nigger narc, or your lazy nephew. They're lost good, by now. They thought I had you! Thought they were saving your ass. They'll never find their way back in time."

His words gave me some hope. Michael would not get lost, not anywhere in the San Luis Valley. The geography of his adopted home was etched in Michael's head like some other people know the way from their bedroom to the bathroom. He could get Reed out of wherever Boudin had led them.

A weathered sign pointed to another road—Grande Vista Rancho, Barber's place. A second sign, in better shape, pointed in the same direction—Sangre de Cristo Water Company.

The dunes rested against the horizon like enormous funeral mounds. They rose hundreds of feet in the thin altitude of the valley. They were a desert in the middle of mountains, shifting piles of sand that could cover the Denver skyline.

In the summer, tourists trekked the back trails, photographed the unique topography, and marveled at the ever-changing shapes, sounds, and colors of the giant sandbox. But now, the visitor center was closed, and the entrance gate shut and locked.

Boudin drove his car off the road and parked it. He got out of the car, walked around the front, opened the passenger door and yanked me outside. He motioned me to walk in the general direction of the dunes.

We walked for a hundred yards along a barbed wire fence until we reached a path that traveled up the dunes. He shoved me against the fence, then growled, "Under it." I crawled in the dirt, ripped my coat, and came up on the other side where I thought of making a run for it. Boudin's rifle erased any idea I had of trying to get away.

The sky began to lighten and the wind picked up. I buttoned my coat. Boudin said, "Run, asshole." He shoved me and

I started to run along the path, but soon I was climbing through a thicket of sagebrush, piñon, and ponderosa. I wanted to stop to catch my breath but Boudin shoved me again. I heard only the wind whistling in my ears, the rustle of pine boughs, and the labored breathing of me and my captor.

We emerged from the thicket onto the edge of the dunes themselves. I walked on sand—soft, pliable sand that shifted beneath my feet. My feet struggled and my legs strained but I kept walking. I moved up, along the edge of the dune. We continued for several minutes. I unbuttoned my coat. Sweat dampened my back and sides. When the cold wind reached into my coat, my wet skin tingled and I shivered. Nothing blocked my view except the dune itself and, off to the east, the Sangre de Cristo Mountains. But immediately around me there was only sand. I was on a hill that should have been in northern Africa. The clatter of a Moroccan marketplace should have drifted to my numb ears. I should have seen signs of Bedouins and camel tracks. But the icy wind could only come from the Colorado high country. The backdrop of Colorado mountains reminded me that I had to confront the possibility of my own death surrounded by frozen wildflowers and faded *chamiso hediondo*.

Boudin growled again, "Sit your ass down."

I stopped and sat on the sand. It moved beneath me. The earth was damp and cold.

Boudin stared into the distance, looking for something or someone. I thought about Medano Creek and how it flowed along the edge of the dunes in the spring and early summer, fed by melting snow. I knew that what kept the sand damp was the high water table, abundant snow melt, and the vast expanse of ancient sea that lay hidden beneath the dunes. Sand ironically marked the source of wealth and power that had driven men like Fermín Santos, Matthew Barber, and Max Macías to the extremes that had culminated in death. Murder. Suicide of the soul.

Boudin paced across the sand. He appeared to be waiting for something. The wind cut me, the sand danced, and the end of the night played eerie tricks on my eyes and mind.

"Why do you hate Mexicans, Boudin? Why do you hate yourself?"

He stopped pacing. He raised his rifle at me. He sighted down the gun and moved his fingers rapidly over the trigger.

"Yeah, you are one smart greaser. Whatever you think you know about me, forget it! Anybody says any different—is dead. Like you're going to be."

He would never explain it to me. He probably couldn't explain it to himself. But we both knew in that instant when he considered me already dead that he was living a lie, and that he would kill to keep that lie intact. His twisted life had twisted how he thought of himself, and how he thought of me, and all those others who reminded him of who and what he really was.

A yellow ray streamed across the yellow dune like a beacon from a lighthouse. The sun threw shadows across the sand that looked like nothing I had ever seen. Jagged, contorted shapes bounced between the sand hills, colors from the grains of sand reflected the last stars and the new sun.

A man's shape split one of the rays. He wore a green parka and thick gloves. He held a gun.

The sun crept up behind him and his features were lost in black shadow.

Boudin aimed his rifle at the man.

The second man moved closer to us and his face became as clear as the icy air. I saw a ghost, a man back from the dead. My surprise must have been obvious because his grin was as wide as Harry Lopez's permanent leer.

I said, "Dominic Santos. You missed your father's funeral."

Anger clouded the details of his face and erased the smile that had reminded me of López. He sagged like a tired man, like a man at the end of a marathon.

Boudin poked his rifle in Santos's side. He said, "Drop the gun, Dominic. It's over."

Santos shrugged. Boudin screamed, "You idiot! You blew it, man! You blew my cover, the whole trip. You were supposed to stay away, to let the feds babysit you. But just like this jerk, you came looking for me. And just like this jerk, you got to die, too, Dominic."

Santos looked at me as he raised his gun. I thought it would fall to the sand. It exploded in Boudin's face. Tyler Boudin collapsed, then swayed on the sand, kneeling as though he was praying. His face and neck were covered in blood. Softly, almost peacefully, he let go of his rifle, rolled backwards and died.

I jumped to my feet and grabbed Boudin's weapon.

Dominic aimed at me. He said, "You're finally getting yours, Móntez. Boudin didn't figure it out. I didn't want only him. He was part of it, a big part, because of what he did. But, I'm finishing the job that Mariele started, that she would have finished if that stupid López hadn't screwed up."

From out of the darkness Michael Torres hollered, "Drop the gun, Dominic! It's over!"

A shot rang out and a cloud of sand erupted near the feet of Dominic Santos. Santos jumped back. He lost his balance on the incline of the dune and the undulating sand. His feet gave way and he fell to his hands and knees. His gun flew from his hand and was lost in sand. Michael ran to us. Santos remained on his knees, shaking his head.

"What the hell you going to do? Shoot me? Go ahead! You think I give a damn? If you don't, the feds take me back to their so-called protection program. You think that's a life? Doing what they want, whenever they want? Pull the trigger, Móntez. Do us all a favor."

Headlights glared across the bottom of the dune. At least two vehicles had stormed up the road and braked to noisy stops. Armed men jumped from the trucks. John Reed led the pack up the dune.

I held Boudin's rifle on Santos and said, "The jail house riot, your phony death. All engineered by Tyler Boudin. All aimed to get you into witness protection, so you could testify against your bosses, against whoever it is that runs drugs through the valley. You faked it all just to get away. Now, you regret it."

He finally made it back to his feet. His dark face was framed with bushy eyebrows and a thick mustache that allowed only a hint of a mouth.

"Boudin was an animal. He killed my father! And . . . Mariele. He burned down Barber's cabin, killed Alarid. Framed me for that so that I'd be picked up, so that he could squeeze me into snitching for him. He used me like a prison bitch. And he did the same to you. You were his partner, whether you knew it or not. You got my father and Mariele killed. You brought death to the valley, Móntez. It followed you down here."

Michael stood a few yards from Santos. His steady hands aimed his hunting rifle at the head of Fermín Santos's heir.

John Reed sweated and huffed to where we stood. Clouds of vapor steamed from his mouth.

"Goddamn, it's Santos! And Boudin . . ." He looked at the bloody corpse. "We lost him, back on the other side of town. We were on his ass since yesterday morning, when he tried to sneak into town, to get to you. We should have taken him, but we wanted him to make a move, seal his finish. Santos showed up and confronted him, then the two of them led us on a crazy chase. We thought they had you. They fooled us. Boudin took us out in the boonies, ditched us like we were kids, left us with flat tires. We lost Santos, too. It took us a while to get back. We rushed out here as soon as we could. Good thing your nephew knew what the hell to do. Damn! You all right, Móntez?"

I dropped the gun. Michael grabbed my arm.

We walked away from a sobbing Dominic Santos and John Reed quietly giving orders to his men. Reed talked to someone on a cell phone.

"Yeah, we got him. We'll bring him back. Boudin's history. Dumb ass thought he could control Dominic through his father, and when that went all to hell he killed them both, the old man and the wife. Yeah, that's Dominic's motive for it all, for walking away from us, for going after Boudin, his old buddy. Maybe we can do something for the poor bastard . . ."

His voice drifted away with the wind, buried by the sand. Below us, a silver SUV idled. A man in an orange hunting vest and a tan Stetson watched us through binoculars. Michael Torres and I waited for the sun to finish rising on the beautiful San Luis Valley. Together we climbed down the face of the sand dune.

EPILOGUE

WINTER HAD SETTLED in with a vengeance. Drifts piled up outside my office door. The temperature didn't sneak past zero for several days in a row. Rosa suffered through a hellish cold, and my business froze like the garden hose I had forgotten to return to the garage.

We sat around her desk drinking coffee and eating hamburgers I had risked life and limb for by making a run to a drive-through over on Broadway.

Rosa sported a red rose tattoo below her neck in a place that almost was immodest. She didn't use the top two buttons on her loose fitting blouse and so I was given a good view of the new ornamentation. I would have lost the bet that I had been willing to make only a few weeks before about the existence of the tattoo. The artwork was new.

She opened her blouse even more to give me a better view as she explained, "I got bored, what with all the snow. It's off the hook, no? What do you think?" She winked, then blew her nose. Her cold had not completely given up.

Diplomatically, I simply said, "Looks fine." Actually, I did kind of like it.

While we ate, Rosa talked about her favorite subject, the tangled lives of Mariele Castilla, Dominic Santos, Tyler Boudin and Harry López. I listened, nodded occasionally when it seemed appropriate, and tried not to dwell on the details of an episode that had infatuated her but that I would have just as soon forgotten.

"Mariele connected with Harry? Really? She liked that guy? I guess she wasn't too choosy."

I let that pass.

"She agrees to help him bring you down, arranges for Emilio to meet Harry, not knowing, of course, that Emilio has his own agenda as far as Harry's concerned. Then, the poor thing ends up dead with old man Santos, killed by Tyler Boudin because she was in the wrong place at the really wrong time. Boudin and Dominic, now that's a pair! One after the other for their own purposes. Boudin needs a snitch, Dominic needs protection but decides to run out on Boudin. That decision only results in the deaths of the old man and Mariele. So, of course, Dominic kills Boudin. Guess Dominic wins that one. If you can call what's left of his life winning. He almost got you, too."

I shrugged. I said, "You think the old man would agree that I earned his retainer?"

She finished her sandwich and threw the remains in a trash can.

"You mean by tripping up his son, the man you were going to defend? That's a hard one, Louie."

I nodded.

"Dominic's faked death could have been uncovered," she offered, "if Mariele or Fermín had checked it out better. She didn't really want to, I guess, and the old man was laid up with his heart thingie. But, who's buried in Dominic's grave?"

I would have been very grateful for a beer to compliment the burger. The acidic coffee had to substitute.

"Probably no one. Or some poor cluck of a stand-in. The DEA's faked death before, they know how to pull it off. They stalled Mariele here in Denver, and then would have been ready for the funeral in the valley. Tyler killed her and saved the agency the trouble."

Rosa was about ready to get back to work. She asked questions about one of my cases, confirmed an appointment for later that day.

Her voice faded. Her image dimmed and the office slipped

away. I thought again about quitting. The cranking furnace heat and the greasy lunch made me drowsy. I could hear the snow falling on the sidewalk outside my office. I could feel the branches of the tree near the front door bend under the weight of ice. My eyes were blinded by the white light of winter. My heart thumped crazily in my chest. I thought of Alicia.

Rosa's voice cracked through my daze. "You okay, Luis? You don't look so good."

I said, "Never better, Rosa. Never better."